THE SCOT

Order of the Broken Blade

1214

CECELIA MECCA

CHAPTER 1

Stokesay Castle, Northumbria, 1214

"Your husband is dead."

That the news made Roysa curious instead of sad said much about her short marriage.

"How?" she asked her brother-in-law, who seemed no more broken up than she felt. Which made her even more curious. Roysa had been married to Walter for less than a year. This man had been his brother for two and thirty years. Surely he should be reacting with something more than a nearly imperceptible lift of his thin brows.

"A hunting accident."

It seemed those were the only details she would receive.

Lord Langham indicated she should sit. The small wooden chair with its velvet cushion might have been inviting if she were in her parents' solar back home. But here, like everything about Stokesay Castle, the seat felt stiff and unwelcoming, much like her late husband. And his brother.

Although Roysa would prefer to retire to her chamber, somewhere she could absorb this surprising news and what it might mean for her, she knew she could not yet separate herself from this foul man's presence. As always, her needs meant little.

"As his widow . . . ," the brother began.

I am a widow.

Roysa had always been in possession of an active imagination, but this was one role she'd never imagined herself playing.

Walter had sat opposite her in this very chamber, chastising her about her "too lenient" treatment of the servants, mere days ago. And now he was dead. The finality of it was shocking.

"Lady Roysa?"

She snapped back to the present. "He is truly dead?"

Langham did not hide his impatience. "I assure you, the death of my brother is not a matter I'd trifle with, my lady. He is, in fact, deceased."

Why are you not upset?

Of course she'd not ask such a question, but it sat there on her tongue like a blackthorn berry, bitter and unfit for consumption.

"You will, as is customary," Langham said, looking at her as if she were the least significant person in the castle, "have forty days to vacate. A dower manor will be arranged."

Roysa had some idea of where he planned to install her.

"Holton Manor?"

Her guess did not please the new baron, the twitch of his brows reminding her of Walter.

"Indeed."

"As per the marriage agreement, you will also receive Holton for a term of one hundred years, along with rent collected from its tenants. Over five hundred marks per year."

Something in his tone gave her pause.

The new baron sounded . . . hopeful. Those were

indeed the terms of the marriage agreement, and though she was glad he planned to honor them, she also knew Holton edged the northernmost border of their land. The border was a tumultuous place at the best of times—and this was most certainly not the best of times.

"Is it safe?" she blurted before realizing she should not have done so. How could she expect an honest answer from the man who'd just delivered the news of his brother's death as if he were discussing the day's weather? She watched his eyes carefully but could glean nothing from him.

"Of course," he said, too smoothly. "If you will pardon me, Lady Roysa."

A dismissal. One she would gladly accept.

Barely conscious of what she was doing, Roysa dragged herself to her bedchamber. Sitting on the bed she'd occupied for the past year, she contemplated what was to come.

What would it be like occupying Holton Manor as a widow? Although she'd dreamed of something very different before her wedding—a happy future here at Stokesay Castle with children and plentiful laughter—it had not taken long for reality to set in. She'd fallen in love with a man conjured by her own imagination. Her handsome husband had been neither honorable nor kind.

Roysa shuddered.

"Lady Roysa?"

Her maid peeked inside, and for some reason, it was the sight of Lisanne that finally brought tears to Roysa's eyes. Although her maid, who was six and twenty, was only her elder by two years, Lisanne had been married, widowed, and married again. She looked after much more than Roysa's wardrobe.

"Why are you crying?" she asked, her gentle tone reminding Roysa of her sister Idalia, which made her cry a little harder. "My lord was a horrible man, God rest his soul. And a much worse husband." oh

Pulling away, Lisanne grabbed a small linen cloth off the bedside table and handed it to her.

"Because I did not do so when Langham told me." Aware she was making no sense, Roysa attempted to explain. "I felt nothing. What kind of woman learns of her husband's death and feels . . . nothing?"

Lisanne planted her hand on her hips. "One whose husband mistreated her. Who refused to allow her to leave, even to visit her sick mother. One who should be thankful his brother despised my lord even more than the rest of us did." uh

Roysa's brows drew together. "Despised? I thought the brothers got on well enough?"

Lisanne's look of pity did not inspire her to make further inquiries.

"You've not heard, then?"

"I came here immediately, and you know none but you will speak freely to me."

Fear had stayed their tongues rather than loyalty. Roysa often wondered how she would have gotten along at Stokesay had Lisanne not taken her into her confidence.

"They're only whispers . . ."

Lisanne hesitated. This gossip, whatever it was, made her nervous, which did not bode well for Roysa.

"Tell me," she insisted.

"'Tis possible they are false rumors, my lady."

She resisted the urge to beg her friend to speak, and instead waited for her to do so.

"'Tis said," Lisanne said, raising and then lowering her shoulders. "'Tis said 'twas no accident. That Langham killed my lord for having relations with his wife."

Roysa simply stared.

Her mother had often reprimanded her for gossiping with the maids, but she'd done so for a reason: the servants were often correct.

Lisanne's worry became her own as she thought back to her short meeting with Walter's brother. Langham had smiled as he spoke of sending her to Holton Manor. That smile had been anything but pleasant.

Although the story was outrageous, she suspected it was true. And she suspected something else— Langham did not plan for her to live comfortably there until the end of her days. He thought to dispose of her as he'd very possibly done with his brother. Title and land and the possibility of power did strange things to men, something Roysa knew all too well.

If she'd thought Walter dangerous, his brother was even more so.

And Roysa would not wait at Stokesay to learn if she was right.

CHAPTER 2

"**A**gain."

Terric ignored the sound of swords clanging around him, focusing instead on blocking his friend's blade as the blunted steel hurtled toward his head.

"The men are near frozen, Terric."

Lance threw this bit of commentary at him as he twisted away from his counterattack.

Sure enough, snow dotted the frozen ground. March at Dromsley Castle, he had found, was as frigid as it was back home.

Though, he supposed, this *was* his home now. Terric had spent more time at his English estate this past year than he had at Bradon Moor. He'd known that would be so, of course, when he and his friends had formed the Order of the Broken Blade, pledging to either dethrone the corrupt King John or force him to desist his worst policies. All four of them, along with the barons and others who had pledged themselves to their cause, had given up something. Relinquishing his home, for now, was a small price to pay.

"The men may soon be fighting for their lives," he

huffed out, taking another swing. "The practice will do them good."

Terric landed a blow against his friend's sword this time, the sound ringing through the training yard.

"Again," he prompted when Lance held up a hand.

His friend's brow crinkled, which was really fair enough. They had been training since the midday meal, and now that darkness began to descend, he supposed their session should soon come to an end.

"Last one," he amended.

As he always did in training, Terric imagined his sister, defenseless, splayed on the ground in front of the man who'd meant to steal her innocence. With a roar, he swung harder than he had all day. Lance deflected him, but he promptly lowered his weapon and held up his hands. This time, he knew his friend would not be waylaid. They were done for the day.

"Idalia will wonder if you finally managed to kill me in training."

Terric sheathed his sword. "Not today." Grinning, he slapped his friend on the back. As always, Lance remained much too serious for his liking. "You look as if the king himself waits at the gate."

The blacksmith-turned-knight sheathed his own sword.

"He may well be at the gate sooner than we think." The Order of the Broken Blade had finally declared their demands to the king several months prior. If he agreed, his tyranny would be at an end—if he did not, they would go to war.

The Order of the Broken Blade and the others who supported their rebellion had spent all winter waiting.

The other men in the training yard began to pack up their things.

"Has Idalia received word from her father yet?"

"Nay. Nothing since the last report. No movement from John's allies has been detected."

The two remained silent as they made their way from the training yard back into the castle. Lance stopped suddenly, pulling Terric to the side.

"John delays too long."

They'd had this conversation so many times over the past months, Terric had nothing new to offer. He agreed. But they certainly hadn't expected the king would immediately accept their demands.

Open rebellion against a king was not supposed to be easy. Or clean. They'd made their demands, and now they waited. And waited.

Dromsley Castle was as prepared as possible, although Terric's clansmen had not yet joined them from across the border in Scotland. They would arrive as soon as the weather allowed for travel.

"'Tis maddening." Lance's jaw ticked. "How can you remain so calm?"

He was anything but.

"We will crush him," Terric said in a tone that made even his hardened friend flinch. "If I am calm, it's because I've been waiting for the moment John, or his men, dare to take what is mine. I look forward to it."

"I worry for Idalia," Lance admitted.

"You're a fool for taking a wife," he said, nodding toward the corridor. He'd said the words any number of times, although there was no heat behind them. They began walking once again, the smell of some kind of roasting meat reminding Terric he'd hardly eaten that day.

"Say as much to Idalia," Lance dared.

"It's as if you conjured her," he said with a grin. Indeed, the very woman they'd discussed had just stepped into the other end of the corridor.

"You will not come into the hall in such a state,"

she called to them, reminding Terric of the many times his mother had chastised him and his brother for entering the hall much as they had today, directly from the training yard.

It still amazed him, the way his friend, the steadfast warrior, changed at the sight of his lady wife. He became a man who smiled easily, spoke gently, and greeted his wife with a kiss. The pair of them had lived with him at Dromsley all winter, so Terric had become accustomed to their antics. And despite what he'd said to Lance, he was very fond of Idalia. It was almost as if his sister were here, with them, rather than back home at Bradon Moor.

"How will Dromsley Castle get on without you when you return to Tuleen Castle?" Terric asked as they reached Idalia. Turning to Lance, he added, "To be clear, I'm speaking of your wife. Not of you."

Lance ignored him.

"You could, mayhap, obtain a wife of your own," Idalia answered sweetly.

He laughed, Lance joining him, until Idalia planted her hands on her hips.

"'Tis not so outrageous as that."

"Aye." Lance placed another kiss on his wife's nose in parting. "'Tis as outrageous as the idea of King John actually arranging a meeting."

"More outrageous," Terric muttered, shaking his head. "We will return."

When they turned to leave, Idalia called back to them. "Clean and changed for dinner."

"You'll miss her," Lance commented as he turned toward the corridor that led to the east tower.

"Indeed," he agreed. He was sorry to see them both leave—and worried for their safety too. Dromsley Castle would not be as easily breached as Tuleen. Although it might not come to a battle. Perhaps the reason for the delay was because the king was considering giving in to the order's demands.

The thought was not a welcome one. He was ready to fight.

He wanted one.

CHAPTER 3

Roysa sighed as she looked down at the ruined hem of her favorite gown. It was as black and muddy as her mood. Nudging her mount forward, she was thrilled to see Dromsley Castle before her but worried at the reception she might receive.

Idalia, please be here.

Though Roysa's last letter from her sister had come from this castle, it was entirely possible Idalia had moved on. Her sister had become much more secretive since meeting Lance. Indeed, she'd never actually explained why she and her new husband had not wintered at Tuleen. Her mother had been nearly as coy in her last missive, leaving Roysa to wonder if something was amiss.

By all accounts, however, Idalia was still wildly in love with her husband, something that pleased Roysa beyond measure. She would not wish her own unhappiness on anyone, especially not her sister.

Langham had not taken kindly to her decision to visit Dromsley. Leaving Stokesay, he'd insisted, was akin to forfeiting her claim as the dowager of Holton Manor. To his mind, she'd do better to make the visit once she was safely established in her new home.

She believed him no more than she trusted the two men he'd sent as her escorts.

Lisanne had urged Roysa to leave without informing the new baron of her plans, but such a feat would be impossible, or nearly so. A woman traveling alone would be in constant danger, a fact she'd considered many times of late. And so she'd declared her intentions to Langham, but she'd taken care to protect herself.

When he'd argued that she should at least delay her trip until the weather cleared, speaking slowly as if she might have difficulty understanding his words, Roysa pretended to be weak. Confused. A stronger woman was more likely to end up on the other side of the baron's spear."

"If I wait, my lord, will my father not come here after me?"

Langham's brow had furrowed then, much like it had after she'd asked him if her husband was truly dead.

"Why would he do such a thing?" he'd demanded.

"I informed him, of course, of the circumstances."

"No messengers have left Stokesay Castle since my arrival," he argued.

"I did send one," Roysa insisted, taking care to make the lie sound true. "The day you returned."

She'd looked up at him with big eyes, feigning stupidity. Mayhap he would be satisfied with getting rid of her—enough so that he would not feel the need to make it a permanent arrangement. Or he might decide he didn't much feel like waiting to murder her and do so then and there.

Instead of brandishing his sword and slicing her open, Langham had merely stared her down. When he finally relented, offering two men to accompany her, Roysa nearly crumpled to the ground with relief.

If she had known then how miserable the journey

would be, mayhap she would have asked Langham to end her torment early.

Idalia would roll her eyes if she ever said such a thing in her presence. Her sister had always been more practical—Roysa was known for being dramatic, or so their mother had always said. Tilly was the baby of the family, still at home with their parents.

Oh, she needed her family. She needed *Idalia*. Besides which, the thought of continuing on to Stanton, her parents' home, with her two unwilling guards was unconscionable. Although the men had not touched her—thank God for that—they hadn't been pleasant companions. She didn't wish to spend several more days and nights in their company.

They approached the gatehouse just before dusk. Roysa hoped the earl, a Scotsman according to her sister, was not as intimidating as his fortress. Concentric and surrounded by a water-filled moat, its inner walls were higher than the outer ones they'd just passed. The four towers, two hugging the sides of the gatehouse and two more at its back corners, looked even taller than the ones at Stanton.

Impressive.

"Dismount and present," one of the guards demanded from above in the tower. Her companions did as they'd been requested. She looked between the two, wondering why they did not take exception to the man's tone.

He'd sneered at them as if they were enemies and barked the orders more forcefully than her husband had ordered her to undress.

"I am Lady Roysa, daughter of the third earl of Stanton." She deliberately left any association with Walter out of her name.

"Dismount," the guard repeated.

She heeded the order this time, feeling rather out

of sorts, but as soon as her boots stepped onto the ground, she realized she was too close to the horse's hindquarters. Either the animal sensed her disquiet or it was merely uncomfortable after the very long journey, for it kicked out, startling everyone present. Another of the castle guards rushed forward, drawing his sword.

Whatever he had intended, all he accomplished was startling the already-skittish horse.

Roysa hurried away from the horse, but the mare shied away from the guard, charging toward her. She dove out of the way, only to slip on the snow-covered ground, her heel catching an errant rock just before she felt her head hit, hard.

Everything went black.

Roysa opened her eyes, the cold creeping up her back.

"Are you injured, my lady?"

She attempted to focus. When she did, Roysa realized it was the surly guard from earlier who addressed her. He sounded almost . . . kind.

"Aye," she snapped, prompting all four men, the guards and her escorts, to look at her as if she were daft. Standing, waving off a hand of assistance, she wondered what prompted the change.

"Her sister will not be pleased," one of the guards said to the other.

How long had she been on the ground? Roysa's hand flew to her hair, and although it had become a tangled mass, it did not appear anything else was amiss. No lump. She looked at her hand. No blood.

Still, she'd apparently been on the ground long enough for them to learn she was, indeed, Idalia's sister.

"She is still here?" Roysa managed. Approaching her now-calm horse, she ran her hand over her flank, attempting to soothe her frayed nerves.

Her head ached. Despite the heavy mantle, every bit of her felt frozen. Numb. She just wanted to get inside the keep—so long as her sister was actually in there. The men were now speaking among themselves, steadfastly ignoring her.

"Is Lady Idalia still here?" she repeated.

The sound of horses approaching from beyond the gates caught her attention, and she realized the portcullis was open.

Still, the men ignored her.

She thought of her husband sitting at the head table, thankfully giving more attention to the serving maid than he did his new wife. His harsh commands. His casual cruelty. And then there was everything she'd suffered since learning of his death. She'd stood before his brother, his murderer, wondering if she might be murdered too. She'd renounced her marital rights. And then she'd spent the last several days in this awful cold.

Something inside of her snapped.

Roysa hardly ever yelled. But right now, she wanted . . . needed these men to hear her.

"I am cold. And wet. My best gown is ruined"— which was, of course, beside the point, but even so . . . "And you refuse to answer a simple question," she screamed, the sound foreign to her ears. "Where is my sister?"

Her throat actually hurt by the time she was finished. But Roysa felt immeasurably better.

And still, neither her escorts nor the guards answered. Their attention, it seemed, had been commanded by someone else. All four of them were staring at an absolutely massive man who'd just ridden through the gates.

The man looked down at her from atop his equally huge horse. His frown was disapproving and judgmental.

"She is inside, my lady."

Roysa disliked him immediately, despite his good looks.

Her father had always said men were either as honorable or as vile as their lord. The guards' boorishness made sense to her now, as this was most definitely the earl.

"Very good," she snapped, finished with rude men for the day.

"Very good indeed," he fairly growled, his voice low and firm. Aye, the earl. No man sat that confidently or spoke that assuredly without an equally lofty title. "Welcome to Dromsley Castle."

"storm seems to be brewing," Lance said. He looked toward the hall's entrance, presumably for his wife.

Who was currently upstairs with the woman who'd just stormed into his castle as if she owned it. He could hardly believe the two women were related. Although he and his brother were different enough—Terric, their sister said, was the more rigid of the two—they had as many similarities as they did differences. But he'd seen none of Idalia's warmth and kindness in her imperious sister.

Though she had all of her beauty, and more even. His immediate response, attraction, appealed even less than the woman herself.

Of course, Lance wasn't speaking about that kind of storm. He was speaking of a snowstorm. One that would again delay the arrival of his men from Scotland.

"If John does attack come spring, we need those men," Lance continued.

It was a conversation they'd had many times over the winter.

"Rory should have sent them months ago," Terric said.

Even so, Terric did not feel keen to discuss his brother. As chief, he could have ordered Rory to do his bidding. Instead, he'd asked for his brother's counsel—and his brother had argued they'd do best to wait for some reaction from John. If he sent the men too soon, Rory had argued, they would be away too long from Bradon Moor. Except the weather refused to turn to spring, and now those men might arrive too late.

In his heart, he knew his brother did not wish to put the men in danger for a war that was not his own. Neither did he, in truth, but nor could he risk losing his mother's English holding, along with all the men and women who lived there. Nor could he risk the order's mission.

"You did the right thing." Lance did not seem capable of looking away from the entrance. Nearly a hundred men sat below them, eating and drinking, the steady murmur of voices oddly comforting, but Lance did not seem to see anything but the stone archway opposite them. Ah, he would indeed miss the pair of them. "If Rory is to lead in your absence, he must be allowed to do so."

"Aye," Terric agreed, "but not at the expense of holding Dromsley."

"'Tis done," he said, lifting his mug and taking a long swig. "Now, we can only wait out the storm."

A flash of blue finally appeared in the archway, signaling that one storm, at least, was upon them.

When his men had come for him earlier to apprise him of some trouble at the gate, the last thing he'd expected was the arrival of Idalia's elder sister. And yet, the sight of her now surprised him even more than that initial shock.

Certainly he'd noticed she was a beautiful woman before, not surprising given her sister, but this woman was . . .

Regal, that was the only word that fit. She looked like a lovely queen—beautiful and untouchable. Her hair was a shade darker than Idalia's, brown like his own. Chin held high, she wore an unusual headpiece, a single jewel falling onto her forehead. Gold and green to match her belt. Her attire was so different from Idalia's simple gown, though both were the same shade of blue.

Even more beautiful than Isobel.

"Terric." Lance cleared his throat.

He'd been staring.

They stood as both women stepped onto the dais.

The sister, a woman who cared for fine gowns. And titles, no doubt. But a damned beautiful one all the same.

"Idalia. Lady Roysa," he greeted them. Why the sister had come without her husband, let alone in the bitter cold of March, Terric neither knew nor cared. She was the sort of woman he despised. Haughty. Entitled. A woman to be endured.

Thankfully, she sat on the other side of her sister, well away from him.

"We apologize for our tardiness," Idalia said, sitting.

"Understandable given the circumstances," Lance offered. Very well, he could act the gracious host this evening. Terric would just as soon turn his attention to the ale in front of him.

"Lady Roysa—" Lance began, although the lady in question cut him off.

"Roysa, if you will. We are brother and sister, after all."

Never had a voice so matched a person's countenance before. Deep, strong. Throaty.

"Roysa, then. But only if you will use my given name as well. Though I'm glad to meet you, the circumstances are . . ."

He didn't seem inclined to finish, so Terric did it for him. "Unfortunate."

Lance shot him a look of surprise, but it was Idalia who spoke. "Terric?"

Her tone was so like his mother's—the rebuke implicit—it nearly made him smile.

But not quite.

"For my lady," he recovered. "To be forced to travel in such conditions."

The look Lady Roysa gave him was not one he'd ever seen from her sister. She leaned forward over the trencher that had been placed in front of her.

"I am sorry for nearly being trampled at your main gate, my lord."

Her emphasis on that last word made him cringe. Aye, haughty indeed.

"It did seem to be a spirited"—he paused apurpose—"animal."

When Lady Roysa gasped, Terric forced his expression to remain neutral.

"Are you referring to me?" she asked.

He could admire her forthrightness, if nothing else.

Liar. There may be at least one, or two, other things to appreciate.

"Lady Roysa, my apologies if I appeared to disparage you in any way."

He waited for her to offer him the use of her given name, as she had with Lance, but she merely lifted her chin higher, if such a thing were possible, and turned away.

Lance was openly glaring at him now, but Terric would not back down. He did not care for the woman, and although he should temper his response for Idalia's sake, he simply could not do it.

Would not do it.

This was no court where every glance or whisper

was studied as closely as Aristotelian philosophy. Dromsley Castle had become a stronghold, one of the seats of the order's incipient rebellion against the king. The castle's fortifications would likely be tested for the first time since his mother's grandfather had built this structure.

It was his duty to protect the men and women of Dromsley, and all else who took shelter here. His duty to ensure both his mother and sister remained safe. Nothing else mattered. Certainly not *her*.

He looked down at his men as he ate, trying not to listen to their new arrival conversing with Lance and Idalia. Her voice penetrated even from three seats away, however, despite the continual hum of voices and occasional shouts for more ale. Lance finally turned back to him. "You're thinking of your sister," he said softly.

"I thought Guy was the one with premonitions?"

His reply had clearly surprised the smith. Guy, another member of their order, rarely spoke of his premonitions—and the rest of them usually honored his forbearance. It struck him that Lance was, of course, no longer a smith. He was a knight, a lord in his own right, but to Terric, he'd always be the young smith he'd met at that tournament so many years ago.

A brother in all the ways that mattered.

"I know more than you think, my friend," he said.

Lance leaned toward him. "Though not, it seems, how to charm a woman."

Terric laughed.

"Charm?" he whispered back. "I can assure you, I have no interest in charming that woman. A married woman," he added, more than a bit confused by Lance's comment.

"You haven't been listening, my friend. Roysa is a widow."

The tankard froze before it touched his lips. Immediately his body responded, forcing him to readjust in his seat. Recovering quickly, he took a long sip. Long enough to regain his composure.

A widow.

Lady Roysa had been married just the year before. Maybe not so much a surprise she'd made haste to her sister. Such a loss must have come as a surprise.

It made her attitude more understandable. Slightly. But she was still a woman very much like Isobel.

Terric leaned forward, prepared to offer his condolences, when the woman in question glared at him. The jewel on her forehead flashed nearly as brightly as her eyes as she stared at him directly, her gaze unwavering.

"No, you may not use my given name," she snapped.

"I hadn't planned to ask," he offered back, realizing he'd had the right of it after all.

Widow or no, Lady Roysa was not a woman he wished to charm. This night or any after it.

In fact, just the opposite.

Terric stood to leave.

CHAPTER 5

"How could you live here with *him*?"

Earlier, after the initial disaster at the gate, Roysa had been escorted into the keep, thrilled she'd not missed her sister. But their reunion had been interrupted by well-meaning servants and a brief visit with Idalia's husband. Now, finally, they were alone together, sitting side by side on the bed in the guest room Roysa had been shown to earlier.

Legs crossed, Roysa pulled the coverlet over her ankles. The bedchamber was warm, courtesy of not one but two fires in each corner of the room. Even so, the chill that had taken hold of her since leaving Stokesay would not abate.

Idalia pulled her robe more tightly around her waist.

"I like him."

Of course she did. Idalia liked everyone.

"I do not."

But she did. In the same way she had liked her husband. Both were very handsome men. The first time, she mistook desire for love. She'd not make the same mistake again.

Idalia's hands reached out, and Roysa instinctively took them.

"Do you remember when we last sat this way?" she asked, her memory of it as clear as if it had happened just yesterday.

"Aye. You were excited to begin a new life." Idalia squeezed her hands. "Tell me what happened."

Part of her wanted to tell Idalia everything. Every sordid detail. But as always, she held something back. There was no point in making her younger sister worry now, when Walter was no longer alive to torment her. "It was as I wrote. All was"—she tried not to choke on the words—"well. But I do believe I mistook desire for love."

Idalia let go of her hands, shifting her weight on the bed.

"All was . . . well?"

She shrugged. "Well enough. Until Walter left to visit his brother. I could not understand why he would make the trip in such poor weather. But I didn't question him."

"You didn't . . ." Idalia cocked her head to the side. "Question him?"

"Nay."

She could understand why her sister seemed confused—the girl she'd been had not hesitated to question everyone and everything.

Avoiding any deeper discussion of her marriage, she continued, "Langham arrived and told me his brother had died in a hunting accident. He did not offer any other explanation, although he did claim he would honor the terms of the marriage agreement."

"Holton Manor?"

"Aye. And its rents. But . . ."

She stopped. Although she hadn't told Idalia anything beyond the essential details of Walter's death, her sister had already guessed something was amiss.

She could see it in her eyes. Perhaps from the tone of her letters. Or from the details she'd omitted this night.

Roysa still wished to protect her sister from the worst of the story, but she had to tell her why she'd come to Dromsley unannounced.

"But there were rumors."

"Of?"

"That Walter had cuckolded his brother. And that his death was no hunting accident."

"'Tis a jest."

"Nay," she said, watching her sister's face.

"He . . . murdered his brother?"

Roysa bunched the coverlet around her feet to get them warm.

"Perhaps."

Idalia shifted again, a nervous kind of movement that said she was thinking. From the way her eyes suddenly widened, Roysa knew what was coming next.

"You were in danger?"

The fear in Idalia's voice was so apparent, she hastened to soothe it, stopping just short of lying. "Likely not. But I dared not take a chance. So . . ."

"Dromsley is closer than Stanton."

"Aye."

"You fled in fear for your life?" Idalia raised her voice with each word.

Attempting to comfort her—and end the discussion—she said, "Nay, of course not. I fled . . . to be safe. So, here I am. And so very tired." She forced a yawn as she continued to rub her feet. The cold refused to leave her, it seemed.

"Oh no, Roysa. Stop it. I am not a child. And you do not need to protect me any longer. In fact, when you learn why we are here . . ."

This time it was her sister who hesitated.

Roysa sat up straighter. "Why *are* you here? Idalia, are you in danger? You said Lance was a good friend of the chief's, and that he was hosting you for an extended stay. . ."

Her words drifted off as Idalia bit her lip.

"Idalia," she said. Although she had not intended to sound quite so matronly, protecting sweet-natured Idalia was something she had done for one and twenty years. Until she had left Stanton to marry.

Well, perhaps not that entire time. She'd only been little more than a babe when her sister was born.

"I am waiting."

Mimicking her, Idalia yawned. "I would not keep you after such a long day. We will talk tomorrow." Bounding from the bed, her sister moved toward one of the dwindling fires. Stoking it, she spoke quickly. Too quickly. "I've arranged for a maid to attend to you. Get some rest."

She turned, and Roysa did not even attempt to stop her. Getting her sister to talk now would be as easy as convincing Langham to admit he'd murdered his brother.

Even so, she couldn't allow her to get away this easily. "We *will* speak tomorrow," she said.

Idalia ignored her tone and smiled as she moved to the door. "I am glad you are here. Safe." But she only closed the door partway before sticking her face through the crack. "And I know 'tis much too soon, but he is not promised."

"He?"

With that, Idalia slammed the wooden door closed.

He is not promised.

She would dearly love to feign ignorance, but only a fool would deny that the only thing unpleasant about the lord of Dromsley Castle was his personality. As for everything else . . .

Nay, she could not deny it to her sister. Surely even a happily married woman could appreciate looking at such a fine man. Aye, he had a disposition none would envy, but he was a handsome brute.

And not promised.

CHAPTER 6

"I love the snow." Idalia had just walked into her room, but she'd paused at the window, looking down at the tufts of white collecting beneath them. It reminded Roysa of their childhood, of the snowstorms they'd played in together, only to run inside and drink warm beverages by the fire.

Oh, she'd missed her sisters.

"As do I," she agreed. "Thankfully, it held off for my journey."

Idalia crossed the room to her. "You missed the morning meal."

"Aye." Roysa and her father had always been the first to rise at Stanton. Of the three daughters, she probably had the closest relationship with him because of all of their early morning discussions. But neither Idalia nor Tilly had ever resented the fact.

"I still cannot believe you're here."

She looked at her sister with fresh eyes. Something had changed about Idalia—and then the truth struck her.

"You are happy." Her sister had told her it was so in her letters, of course, but now she was seeing it for herself.

Idalia smiled. "Aye, very much so. You will adore Lance as much as I do."

Roysa already liked him. The former blacksmith looked at her sister in a way she'd never seen her parents look at each other. And they'd had a long, mostly happy union.

But their love was the kind that grew from companionship, from being forced together. Her sister's was a different kind of love entirely.

She hugged her then, so very happy that Idalia, at least, had not been fooled about the man she was marrying. If only one of them could have happiness, she would have gladly given it to her sister. Closing her eyes, she rested her head on Idalia's shoulder.

When Roysa finally pulled away, she allowed her sister to wipe an errant tear from her cheek.

"'Tis I who should be caring for you."

Idalia turned back to the window. "You've done so for many years. But with mother's illness . . ."

Roysa winced, anger at Walter bubbling inside her. He'd pretended to care for her, but the illusion had faded quickly. No man who truly loved a woman would not allow her to visit her gravely ill mother. She could never forgive him for that. Dead or nay.

"It was not your fault."

She disagreed but knew better than to say so. "I should have been there," she said simply.

Idalia reached out to touch the glass. "Your duty was to marry."

Roysa placed her fingers above her sisters, pressing the pads to the cold glass. "Father would never agree to such an expense."

They both dropped their hands at once.

"Nay. He would sooner incur the expense than agree to allow you a choice of suitors." Idalia looked straight at her. "You never had a choice, and because of it, convinced yourself you were in love with

Walter. I'm sorry for it, but please do not blame yourself. For mother, for your marriage. For any of it."

"Not even for feeling relief at Walter's death?" She let the words hang between them.

"Not even for that." There was no surprise in Idalia's voice—she'd guessed at her feelings if not the reason for them.

They watched the flakes cover the castle walls, the ground below.

"So . . . why are you here?" Roysa asked.

Idalia took a deep breath as if preparing for a long story. "You know how many of the barons, including father, are displeased with the king?"

"Of course." She probably knew as well as anyone her father's opinion of King John. Of the cruel taxes that had forced some of his people to give up their ancestral land. Of his failed campaign at Bouvines, a battle none of his men had wanted. Her father had said it was King John's single worst decision—one that ensured some of his staunchest supporters would desert him.

"Opposition has been gathering for months. An order of knights was formed. Lance, Terric, and two men you have not met."

Unbidden, the chief's face flashed before her. She pushed it firmly aside.

"You'll have heard of the Earl of Licheford."

Roysa thought for a moment. "Aye, but I know very little about him."

"And the other is a mercenary. Guy Lavallis."

"The swordsman?"

Idalia appeared confused. "You know of him?"

She nodded. "Father mentioned his name before. After the last Tournament of the North, I believe."

"Which is where they met, years ago. The four of them have been gathering support, and last fall, they met with some of the other barons who felt the same way. And they all swore allegiance to one another."

Roysa's eyes widened. The meaning of what her sister had just told her finally penetrated.

"Do you mean . . . ?"

"Aye. An allegiance against the king."

"But . . . 'tis treason."

Idalia did not seem overly bothered at all by the fact that her husband was one of the leaders of a plot against the king.

"Idalia . . ."

"There's more."

This is why the tone of her missives had been so suspicious. Roysa had been too bent on keeping her own secrets to press her, but that had clearly been a mistake.

"They have father's support. Along with some other very powerful men, including the archbishop of Canterbury. After swearing their allegiance to the cause, the archbishop brought a message on behalf of the order to the king, demanding a meeting."

Roysa did not know what to say.

"He was furious, of course. Imprisoned the archbishop and two of Lord Noreham's men. They are out now but . . ."

Roysa was stunned into silence.

"But?"

"He *did* agree to treat with them come spring. None of us know if he plans to honor his word or"—she cleared her throat—"or if he is planning to move against those who defy him. Perhaps he merely wished for more time to assemble his men. But the rebellion began in the north, so if John decides not to negotiate, likely he will begin here as a show of force in one of the north's more fortified strongholds associated with those who defy him."

Roysa's hands flew to her cheeks. Her sister was

31

married to one of the leaders of a revolt against the king. "This is why you are not at Tuleen?"

Her sister nodded once.

"How could Father have possibly allowed this?"

Idalia's look held a warning. One Roysa was inclined to ignore.

"He allowed it because it was my will to be here, with Lance."

"Does John know the identity of the order?"

"He does."

"And you believe he may come against them."

"Us. Come against us."

She liked this less and less.

"Idalia . . . you are in danger."

"As are you. Which is why you cannot stay here. As soon as the storm passes—"

"No." She used her best big-sister tone this time. "I will not leave you." Roysa pursed her lips, waiting for Idalia to contradict her. Thankfully, she did not.

"The king knows the identity of most, if not all, of the rebels. His response so far has been tempered, aside from FitzWalter's imprisonment, and he released him before too long. 'Tis said he did so for fear of the pope's reaction."

"Does the pope support John or the rebels?"

Idalia frowned. "John. But only after the king pledged himself to the Crusade. Still, his rule is so detested, the pope's support has had less influence than we assumed it would. None of the barons who pledged their support have withdrawn it. There's hope the king will do as he says and treat with them in the spring."

Roysa shook her head. "He is delaying."

"Aye. Which is why I am here and Guy Lavallis and his wife are with Conrad at Licheford."

In response to her questioning look, Idalia explained further. "We are preparing for a possible attack."

"Saint Rosalina" she exclaimed, earning a disapproving look from her sister. "I cannot say I was expecting all of this."

A pounding at the door interrupted them.

"Lady Roysa?" a voice called.

"Or him. 'Tis the lord, is it not?"

Idalia nodded. "Though I cannot imagine what would bring him to your door at this hour. And he sounds angry."

After all she'd learned, Roysa was a mite angry herself. Her sister had embroiled herself in a plot against the King of England. She'd dearly love to know how a blacksmith had earned a pivotal role in such a plot.

But first she had to deal with the brute on the other side of the door.

CHAPTER 7

"How may I be of assistance, my lord?" Roysa said, letting more than a touch of ridicule flavor her voice. "Or do I call you chief? 'Tis so rare to meet a man with both titles."

"Roysa," Idalia hissed behind her.

"I would speak with you a moment, my lady."

"Be kind," Idalia said, pushing her way out of the room.

"You're not staying?" she asked, eyeing the rude, though admittedly handsome, man standing at her door. She hated the way he looked back at her, with disdain that should be reserved for someone who deserved it.

Her sister did not seem overly concerned about leaving her alone. With him. Unchaperoned. Did she not realize one of them would be likely to leave the conversation bloody? Did she care so little for Roysa's reputation?

Of course, she was a widow, so her innocence was no longer of great concern.

"I must speak to Lance," Idalia said, only pausing long enough to deliver her explanation.

With that, Roysa was well and truly abandoned.

She looked up to meet Terric's very brown eyes.

"Inside."

When he attempted to guide her back into the bedchamber, Roysa was reminded of the first time her heartbeat quickened when Walter stood so close to her. Of course, he was anything but the courteous gentleman he'd presented himself as before their wedding. Her opinion had ceased to matter as soon as she became the lady of Stokesay Castle.

Never again would she be fooled by a man's visage.

She refused to move from the doorway. "I would prefer to speak here, my lord."

He attempted to guide her backward again. It was no firm push but enough of a nudge that she stumbled slightly.

"My lady, please," he said, his fingers wrapping around her upper arm. To save her from falling? To ensure she understood who was the master here?

It did not seem to matter. He'd already nudged Roysa into the bedchamber, and he stepped away to shut the door. That done, he strode right past her and stood directly in front of the larger of the two fires.

"You will get us killed."

Roysa rolled her eyes but did not move.

"Killed, standing in the corridor? Do you fear we will be done in by an errant stampede of servants?"

Was that a smile?

Nay. She just could not see his face clearly from such a distance. Roysa moved a bit closer.

"By inviting the enemy to stay within our walls."

He grabbed the fire iron, though the maid had already tended to the fire just before Idalia's arrival.

"The enemy?" She took another hesitant step toward him.

"Langham's men."

When he turned, she noticed the way the tips of his dark hair brushed his shoulders. Though clean-

35

shaven, Terric Kennaugh was not a polished lord. At least one of her questions had been answered. She knew what to call this man with two titles. He was more Scots clan chief than English earl.

"They are the enemy?"

There was much, it seems, she did not know.

"Did your sister speak to you about . . . the king?"

That was one way to discuss the matter.

"You mean, the rebellion? Of which you are one of the leaders?"

Ah, there was the scowl. She'd almost missed it.

"It seems she did. So you understand the stakes."

"Aye, very much, Chief."

She took another step toward him, drawn forward by a force she did not altogether understand.

"Then you know your brother-in-law—"

"Former. That man is no relative of mine."

Roysa stood just next to him. And though the bedchamber was massive, it seemed smaller than it had before. It was not unusual to receive guests in such a style, and Roysa hadn't given it much thought. Until now.

"Former brother-in-law, then." There it was again. He didn't smile, exactly, but the corners of his mouth lifted ever so slightly. It dropped as soon as he began speaking again. "While your late husband remained neutral in this conflict, Langham has not."

"How do you know?"

His look would make a weaker woman's knees buckle. This man was supremely confident in his abilities. Or his knowledge. Maybe both.

"We've suspected. But the confidence with which he claimed the barony, even after apparently murdering his own brother, suggests he is firmly John's man."

"You know about that?"

Although she'd not told her sister to keep the information to herself, she hadn't expected it to get back to him so quickly.

"I know everything that happens inside these walls."

"Everything?"

He raised his brow, indicating he took it as a challenge. Good. She'd meant it as one.

"*Everything.*"

Ugh.

"Then you'll know why I would like you to leave this chamber. Thanking you, of course, for your hospitality in offering it to me."

"You are very welcome, Lady Roysa," he said, his tone suggesting otherwise. "And aye, I can guess. 'Tis likely the same reason I am glad to leave it."

He began to do just that and then turned back.

"I have asked your escorts to leave. If you do happen upon them before they do so, kindly do not give them any information."

Did he think her an idiot?

Apparently so.

"You mean I should not tell them to report to their lord that Dromsley Castle is home not just to its ill-tempered earl, but also to key players in a rebellion against the king?"

He looked as if he would murder her.

"Good day, *Lady* Roysa."

"Good day, *Chief.*"

Then, thankfully, he was gone.

CHAPTER 8

C old, wet, and interminably restless after training, Terric made his way toward the keep. Instead of turning toward the North-east Tower and main hall, something caught his at-tention.

She was lost.

"My lady?"

About to comment as he might have had Isobel been standing before him, something in her expres-sion stopped him.

Scared.

Lady Roysa was scared, and he liked it not.

"I want to show you something," he said carefully.

Though she continued to watch him, Idalia's sister said nothing as they continued past the mostly empty inner ward toward the stables. After greeting the marshal, Terric led her straight through to the middle tower.

Opening a small door, Terric stepped inside.

"A storeroom?" she guessed.

A good supposition. Crates and wooden boxes lined the cold, stone-walled chamber.

"Aye."

Terric sat on a rope-handled chest. Roysa did the same.

"It was my mother's private chamber once. She was raised here."

This time, he could tell he'd truly surprised her. He tried to remember not all women who wore the finest silks were conniving liars.

"So far from the hall?"

Terric pointed to the wall, waiting for Roysa to see it.

"A . . . is that a secret passageway?"

He smiled, thinking of the few times he'd been through that door. "Aye. The only one in the castle, that we know of. Which was why my mother stayed here while in residence."

His hands balled into fists.

"King Henry once took Dromsley for his half-brother. My grandmother was devastated. This had been her home. Built by her grandfather."

Why am I telling her this?

"The dispute raged for years. Lord Longespée never set foot inside this castle, never met the people here, but the king had given it to him all the same."

"Aye."

"He always had an excuse not to visit the land. First it was an illness. Then his presence was needed at court. All knew he simply had no patience to grant the people an audience or support them in any way, but it mattered naught. The lordship remained Longespée's, through Henry, and although he didn't care to visit the tenants, he had no problem levying scutage from them."

"My father never did care for him. The king, I mean. Or his protégé."

Perhaps both daughters agreed. The fact warmed him toward her, if just slightly.

"It was a difficult time for everyone, not only my

family, but also the people of Dromsley. When my grandfather finally did wrestle control of the earldom back, an unusual ruling against the king himself, he worried Longespée, or even Henry, might resort to other methods to regain control, even if it was in defiance of the courts."

"And so he built that passageway as an escape."

"For my grandmother. Aye. My mother enjoyed using it for play, as did my siblings and I later on. But its purpose was not for two generations of children's enjoyment."

He waited for her to make the connection.

"You think John is delaying."

Terric wished he knew for certain. And though he knew Idalia had told Roysa everything, 'twas odd, still. Speaking so openly with a stranger.

A stranger that made him oddly comfortable to speak freely.

"'Tis likely. His father favored the tactic."

Roysa shook her head, although not in disagreement, and covered her face with her hands. He had been preparing for this, for the possibility John's promised meeting did not happen—that he had, indeed, been assembling men to attack them.

"He is a bastard, with bastard blood." It may have been the father and his men who'd personally wronged their family, but the son was no better.

"Is that why your father came here so rarely?"

Terric was sure of it. "I believe so. He always thought my mother safer with his people than hers."

"My sister is in danger here as well."

He hated that it was so. And noticed she did not account for herself, thinking of Idalia instead. "Safer here than at Stanton or Tuleen."

Realizing he'd already said too much, Terric stood, taking off both gloves and rubbing his hands together. He needed a fire.

"The day you arrived—"

"My husband died. Was killed by a man I know is despicable. I believe I was lucky to leave Stokesay alive."

"'Tis a mark of your bravery and ingenuity that you did so."

Maybe not so much like Isobel, as neither quality could be associated with the only woman he'd ever loved. And who had confessed to caring more for his brother. Unfortunately for Rory, he'd been born minutes after him. Both their Scottish and English inheritance forfeited to his older brother.

They should not be alone here. The look she gave him now could get both of them into trouble. They left the building, both somber.

But there was no help for it. A fight was coming to them, Terric was certain of it.

Unfortunately, he was less certain they were ready. Not for the fight that may be coming. Nor for the woman with whom he'd shared more than intended.

CHAPTER 9

Roysa had always hated chess.

She'd become fairly good at the game after learning it from her father, but she had one serious downfall—her mind tended to wander. As it was doing now.

After stumbling into the earl, Idalia had given her a tour of the castle. It was easy enough to navigate, the concentric design had taken them in what was essentially a large circle. From the Northeast Tower, above which the great hall was located, to the North Gatehouse, which led out to the training yard, all the way around to the South Gatehouse, where she'd arrived the day before.

She'd been awful, really, and should have apologized to the chief earlier. Anyone with a heart would understand—it had happened after a long journey made necessary by the fact that her brother-in-law possibly meant her harm. All of this after learning her husband was dead. She'd tried to explain but should have said those two simple words. *I'm sorry.*

That he was even more handsome, more virile, than her husband was certainly not the man's fault.

"You're not making a move."

Roysa sat back in her chair before the hearth. The

hall was mostly empty now with the exception of a few servants. Most of the men were out training with Lance and Terric, who had apparently left her to join them once again.

"Do they train all winter?" she asked, shivering at the mere thought of standing outside all day in the cold.

"They do now." Idalia pushed away from the board, sitting back in her own wooden high-backed chair. "With all that is happening around us."

Roysa lowered her voice "Do you think John will order an attack?"

She did not make mention that the earl seemed to think 'twas likely.

Idalia appeared thoughtful. "'Tis possible," she said after a moment. "There are many rumors that he plans to deal with the rebels by taking away their land and titles."

"Which is tantamount to an attack."

"Aye," Idalia admitted. "Though a contingent of Terric's clansmen are coming soon. The weather is not on our side, but with any luck, they will arrive before it is too late. Though Dromsley is heavily fortified, it is lightly garrisoned. Terric usually spends most of his time in Bradon Moor. In his absence, his second, his brother Rory, fulfills that role."

"How did a Scot become earl here at Dromsley?" Roysa asked despite knowing the answer. But saying so would force her to admit she'd become too curious about him.

"His mother's inheritance. His father, the former chief of Clan Kennaugh, married her after they met at the Tournament of the North. When he died, Terric was made both chief and English earl. Though he wishes to offer one of those roles to his brother when he shows signs of having matured, as Terric said. But for now, he fills both roles well."

"I beg to differ."

It was easier to pretend to hate him than to admit she'd allowed herself to be charmed so easily. Again.

Idalia eyed her suspiciously. "You do not like him."

"Nay," she said. "I'm surprised you do."

Idalia cocked her head to the side. "I'm surprised you do not."

They were at a standstill, disagreeing about their host as they did on many things. Somehow they'd always managed to remain close despite their differences—or maybe because of them. But as Roysa looked at the chessboard, one thing became very clear. She leaned forward over the board, moving one of the game pieces. "Checkmate."

"How?" Idalia inspected the move and frowned. "Every time. How do you manage it?"

Roysa did not answer. But the women knew it was the time she'd spent with their father that had given her such an edge. "They are well?"

She did not have to specify who she meant. Idalia knew she would have returned home had she been able.

"Aye. Aside from this rebellion, all is back to normal at Stanton."

"That is some kind of an aside. Idalia, I wish you were not embroiled in this."

Idalia did not appear concerned. "'Tis the right thing to do."

A serving maid walked by, and her sister asked for wine. The normalcy of the request almost made Roysa laugh. They were discussing rebellion while they played chess and sipped wine. Even so, Roysa was glad for it when it arrived. It was of excellent quality, and she said so.

"For its remoteness, Dromsley has done well," she continued.

"I graciously accept the compliment."

The voice belonged to her host. She would have known he was coming had Idalia reacted in any way to his approach, but her sister had not. No doubt she'd controlled her expression, knowing Roysa was likely to make her excuses rather than speak with the chief.

She would not know Roysa may have softened toward him. Acknowledging he made her breath quicken did not mean she would be forced to consider him as anyone other than the dear friend of her brother-in-law.

Without turning, she mumbled, "Chief."

"You may call me by my given name," he said, not for the first time.

"Very well, my lord."

Why did she continue to goad him?

He pulled up a wooden chair between them as if they were old friends. He did not sit in it, however, but stood behind it, laying his arms across the back.

"Is she always as such?" he asked Idalia.

He knew well she was not. Roysa had been extremely courteous when he'd shared his story earlier that day.

Her sister looked back and forth between the two of them. "Nay. I do not know what's come over her."

"The object of your conjecture is sitting betwixt you," she reminded them.

It struck her that the chief was freshly dressed. She noticed other things as well but did not wish to dwell on them.

"Has your afternoon training session ended so soon?" Idalia asked.

This time, the voice from behind her was a welcome one. "Terric finally relented for the day when the snow began to fall in earnest," Lance said.

When he came into view, he leaned down to capture Idalia's hand, which rested on the carved handle of her chair. The little signs of affection between them were still sweet to behold, but Roysa worried for her sister. Part of her wished she'd fallen in love with a less dangerous man. Or that they were both spinsters back in Stanton.

"You've finished with your game?" Lance looked at the board. "Well done, Roysa."

She smiled at her brother-in-law. "Thank you. Do you play?"

"I do and will challenge you to a match, perhaps this evening." He gently lifted Idalia's hand from the arm of the chair. "At the moment I plan to abscond with my wife." He stopped short of saying where they would abscond to, but Roysa had a feeling she already knew.

Idalia grinned, making Roysa suddenly feel like the younger sister. So she truly found pleasure in the act? For there was no mistaking Lance's intent.

"If you will pardon us?"

Roysa stared after them, unable to become accustomed to the idea. Her sister . . . her younger sister . . . was a wife in truth.

Startled from her reverie by the sound of the chief's chair scraping against the floor despite a layer of rushes, she asked, "I don't believe I invited you to sit, chief."

That she continued to push him away was no longer out of desire to do so, but necessity.

"I don't believe I need permission to sit in my own hall. And here, in England, it is lord." He grinned. "Or Terric, if it pleases you."

Roysa's eyes narrowed. "Why are you being so polite?"

"I am always polite." He waved his hand to summon the maid. "To women."

So he was one of *those* men. Very much like Walter, as she suspected. Her husband's roving eye manifested very shortly after their exchange of vows.

This man's looks and status would likely have ladies similarly scrambling to make a match with him. It was surprising he wasn't already married.

"How very courteous of you."

"A flagon of wine, if you please," he said to the maid. She was young, no more than five and ten. Curtseying, the young girl scrambled off.

Roysa caught him staring at her—the kind of penetrating look that made her feel as if she'd peeled off her gown little by little. Ugh. Definitely that kind of man.

"I've been somewhat relentless with the men. We've agreed to give them an afternoon of rest"—he nodded toward her goblet—"so I may as well do so in truth."

Their eyes caught.

And much as she wanted to deny it, Roysa's pulsed quickened.

"Your wine, my lord."

"Many thanks," he said as the maid placed both the flagon and an additional goblet on the chess table between them.

So he was courteous to his servants. Walter had been very much the opposite.

"A fine gown," he said, pouring wine for both of them.

Roysa looked down, her fingertips tracing over the bodice of her kirtle, the lovely cream fabric shot through with gold. She knew what he thought of her. This man considered her fanciful. Vain.

"Stanton is a market town," Roysa said softly. "The first time I accompanied my parents to market, I had not yet seen ten summers. In my rush to see the very first stall as I dismounted, I fell headfirst into the mud."

She took a sip of wine, remembering the yellow gown that she had completely ruined. "A fabric merchant took pity on me and handed my mother the most beautiful yellow damask. My first market day had ended promptly, my father escorting me back to the castle."

Roysa sighed. "He can be a difficult man, my father. But I've always understood him. He feels the weight of all the people who rely on him for their livelihood. You may be surprised to hear that's one of my favorite memories from childhood. I will never forget riding back to the castle with the man I so idolized, the beautiful fabric tied to the back of his mount. A powerful border baron, reduced to escorting his daughter in her muddy gown." She shrugged. "He always seemed more . . . human after that. We turned that damask into my first May Day gown, and I've had a weakness for fine gowns ever since."

Something in his expression had changed. It struck her that he might be thinking of his own father, the one whose roles he now occupied. She knew little about him from Idalia, only that they had been quite close.

"I am sorry about your father," she said.

"As am I. He was a fine man and chief. Beloved by all."

"It must be difficult to fill such a role. Or roles. Chief. Earl. How do you do it?"

Refilling his goblet with wine, the chief—and earl —swirled the deep red liquid in his cup.

"It is my life now."

Roysa turned to the fire crackling beside them. The hall was completely abandoned now—the midday meal had long since ended, but supper was still a ways off. Though the common space was not as large as one would expect in a castle of this size, it was nevertheless comfortable, clean and well maintained with tapestries on every wall. The steward was obviously a capable man.

At Stokesay, the steward, like most of the servants, had been afraid of Walter courtesy of his poor treatment of them. Their work, not surprisingly, had reflected as much.

"And the rebellion."

Roysa looked up. There it was again, that look of interest. Of possibility. It had been a long while since Roysa had been noticed and admired as a woman. That look forced her to remind herself she was newly widowed.

And that the man sitting across from her was even more handsome than Walter had been. Her reaction, stronger.

"They are one and the same."

His voice was so deep, so full of resolve. The tone suggested the words were significant to him, although she did not understand how or why.

"How do you mean?" she blurted out.

She almost wished she hadn't asked. Pain had flickered in his eyes, there and then gone.

"A long story."

Roysa waved her arms around the hall. "It seems we've naught but time today."

"One you don't wish to hear." Lifting his goblet, he offered a toast. "To not murdering each other, Lady Roysa."

She hesitated then relented. Langham was enough of an enemy—she did not require more. She'd be staying here for a fortnight, at least. Best to make peace when it was offered.

"Roysa," she replied.

And then he smiled. A slow, lazy, sensual smile that made Roysa wonder if her sister had been right about him all along. Perhaps her view of him had been too narrow. Her father was a difficult man at times too, was he not? She understood his sharp edges had been rendered so by his responsibilities. Could that not be true of Terric as well? And he had two properties to guide and manage, not just one. Besides, she *had* been a bit awful on that first night.

He continued to smile. Not a complaisant or polite smile, but one that sent a flutter from her stomach to her very core.

"To new beginnings, my lord."

They both finished their wine, placing the goblets on the table at the same time.

"Terric. My name is Terric."

CHAPTER 10

I t was only when the hall began to fill again that Terric realized how much time had passed.

He rarely, if ever, spent a day away from training, but Lance had convinced him to boost the men's morale by giving them a rest. To be fair, the snow was falling in earnest.

When he'd first spied Lady Roysa at the chess table, Terric had very nearly turned away. He'd much prefer to swing a sword, even in the snow, than to converse with his guest's sister. Even if she had been nothing but pleasant earlier. But Lance had pushed him forward, urging him to let bygones be bygones, and he'd agreed to at least put forward a civil greeting.

Then something had compelled him to sit with her.

Maybe it was the way she looked at Idalia, so unlike how she looked at him. No one could question the love and warmth in her eyes. It suggested there was more to her than he'd thought. It suggested—nay, it confirmed—he'd been harsh in his judgment of her. His mother and sister both would have words for his rudeness. His prejudice had sprung from his dealings with Isobel—a woman who had captivated him despite her finery and pretty manners. Her excesses had made him think of Isobel's taste for finery. For her desire to nab the clan chief for her very own. Even still, he had fallen for her.

The price of her treachery etched onto his very soul.

But there was more to Lady Roysa than her taste for pretty gowns, more too than the occasional sharp tongue she'd wielded against him. Watching her with her sister, the two of them regarding each other with such love and mutual affection, had stirred something in him.

Nay, not something.

He'd actually grown hard in the middle of the damned hall as he watched Roysa's full lips part, as he watched her smile and laugh. He could admit now, some time later, that sitting down with her had been the only good decision he'd made of late.

"You're still here?" Lance made little attempt to hide his shock.

Terric gestured for him to sit in the empty chair opposite Roysa. "Join us."

If his friend was surprised, he had good reason to be. Terric rarely drank as much as he had this afternoon, and besides, he'd made it abundantly clear what he thought of Idalia's sister. He could admit his faults, however, and one of them had been assuming the worst of Idalia's sister.

"I assume Terric does not typically dally in such a manner?" Roysa asked with some amusement.

Lance continue to appear bewildered.

"Nay. Never."

She sat forward, as if interested. "Why?"

Before Lance could answer, Terric asked, "Where is Idalia?"

They'd known each other for long enough that he did not expressly need to ask his friend to change the topic. Lance understood his meaning. He told them of the conversation they'd had with the cook and his desire to attempt a mutton pie. Idalia had always taken an interest in the foods being served at Stanton, and she was apparently still in the kitchen, where they'd spent much of the afternoon.

"In the kitchen?" Terric could not resist teasing his friend. This was the same man who'd once hardly known the light of day. So dedicated was he to his craft, he'd all but slept in the smithy before meeting Idalia. Spending the day in the kitchens was not typical behavior for Lance, any more so than Terric spending the day in front of a fire.

Drinking fine French wine.

With a beautiful woman.

Aye, it would seem neither of them were themselves today.

"This is what the blasted weather is doing to us."

"Said like a man who's spent his life wielding a sword and ordering others about." Roysa wiggled in her seat. Terric tore his gaze away from the deep vee of her gown.

"I take it you've experience with such men," he answered dryly.

"My father despises the winter months. Much like you. Though my husband did not seem to be afflicted with such a distaste for shortened training hours."

"I don't despise them. But this winter has been rather harsh. We've much to accomplish before the weather changes."

Roysa cocked her head to the side. "'Tis strange. Lord Ulster said nearly that exact same thing. That it has been a particularly harsh winter."

Terric froze at the name. Lance did the same.

"Did I . . . have I said something wrong?"

Leaning forward, Terric replaced his goblet on the

table between them. Blood pounded through his temples.

"Where did you see Lord Ulster?"

But he already knew the answer. Given the very weather they'd discussed, it was unlikely Roysa had traveled anywhere but Stokesay in recent months.

"Just before Walter left for . . ." She swallowed hard. Reminding him that her husband had died very recently. And he sat here staring at her breasts.

"Just before he left for his brother's manor."

Where he had been killed. Murdered, more like. If the bastard had truly had relations with his brother's wife, Terric thought he'd gotten exactly what he deserved, although Roysa might not thank him for saying so.

Had her husband mistreated her?

He wanted to know.

But he needed to know about Ulster more.

"Do you know why he was there?" Lance asked.

"Nay. He visited for just two days before leaving with Walter."

"He went with him to Langham less than two months ago?"

"I'm . . . I'm not sure. What is wrong?"

Ulster was here, in the north. He'd likely met with Langham.

They needed to move. Now.

Terric stood abruptly, exchanging a look with Lance. "We can't talk here."

Though they were in the most secluded spot in the hall, it was quickly filling up with servants. They risked being overheard.

Roysa looked startled. She clearly didn't understand why they were upset, what her revelation meant to the order. He couldn't explain to her. Not now. "I'm sure you need to refresh for dinner, my lady?"

She nodded once and did not repeat her question.

"Do you need an escort to find your chamber?" Lance said, courteous as always.

"Nay, but thank you, Lance."

Consumed by the need to find and notify his marshal, Gilbert, Terric nodded in parting and began to walk away.

After taking a few steps, he broke into a run.

❦

"ROYSA?"

She groaned at the sound of Idalia's voice, rolling over to bury her face in her pillow.

"Two mornings, she sleeps through the morning meal. If Mother were here—"

"If Mother were here, she would chastise you for causing your dear sister such pain."

The bed sank beneath Idalia's weight as her sister sat behind her.

"Pain?"

Roysa clutched both sides of her head, turning toward the sound. She opened her eyes, groaning.

"'Tis as I thought," Idalia said with a small smile. "Sit up."

Though she complied, Roysa could not help but give her sister the look Idalia had always called the Scaring Stare. When they were younger, this very stare would have sent Idalia running for their mother to complain about her cruelty. In truth, Roysa knew she'd been unkind to her younger sisters on occasion, something she hadn't realized until after she'd left home. She'd missed them so fiercely, it had made her feel empty inside.

Her admiration for her father had been such that she'd occasionally tried to emulate him as a child—to make her sisters fall into line as if they were her servants. It hadn't taken long for her to learn that his way was not hers. Although he did quite a good job of terrifying others into submission, she had no wish to do the same.

"Do not look at me that way. I have something for you. Something that will make you feel better."

Idalia handed her a silver cup. She sniffed it and smiled at the familiar smell. Their mother had suffered terrible head pains for years, so she and her family had had occasion to learn the various methods used to relieve such discomfort.

"I smell willow bark." She took a sip, savoring it, then asked, "How did you guess?"

Idalia propped up a pillow behind her head.

"The first day you met Walter . . ."

Roysa took another sip, praying reverently the remedy would work.

"I was so nervous," she offered, finishing Idalia's sentence. "Mother did warn me about consuming too much wine, but I didn't heed her."

"And you woke up the next morning feeling much the same as you likely do just now."

Her head hurt too much for her to nod. "Aye."

"But you did not care, if you'll remember."

"Because I was in love." She said it softly, almost wistfully.

How lovely it had all seemed. Now, of course, she understood that a person could not fall in love after one meeting. But Walter had been handsome in a very proper sort of way. He'd been charming too, when it suited him, and she'd let her fancies carry her away. They would have a passionate relationship, she'd told herself, one so much deeper than the quiet, loving companionship shared by her own parents.

If only she'd known. That kind of companionship would have been a blessing.

"Or believed it was so," she clarified.

Idalia got up to stoke the fire, much as she had

the previous morning. It was a strange sort of comfort, having her younger sister care for her instead of the reverse.

"You've told me little about what happened, Roysa," Idalia said so quietly Roysa barely heard her from across the chamber.

It was said gently, not a rebuke but an invitation to speak. Idalia wanted to know her story, but she wouldn't press her. And Roysa did not feel inclined to share her burden. Besides, there was nothing extraordinary to tell. The truth was simple enough: the charming suitor she and her parents had met did not really exist. Walter had been a man who cared only for his own selfish desires. His own people had barely mattered to him. She'd not been at Stokesay Castle for long before Roysa realized she had more friends there than he did.

He had not struck her, a fact one of the maids had said she should be grateful for. And she supposed it was true. Still, it seemed such an odd thing, to go from believing you loved your husband to praying he would not visit you at night, all in less than a sennight.

As the pounding in her head began to abate, if only slightly, her stomach reminded her she'd not eaten since yesterday's midday meal.

"I would dearly love to break my fast."

Idalia opened the trunk at the foot of her bed. She'd taken little from the castle, for Langham had not allowed them to take a packhorse. "Will this do?"

"Aye," she said. The yellow kirtle a simple one, more akin to Idalia's typical style than hers. "What happened yesterday?"

She got up from the bed slowly, and Idalia helped her dress. Growing up, they'd often assisted each other in lieu of a maid. A practice heartily frowned upon by their very proper mother.

"After you found your bedchamber and fell upon your bed, fully clothed?" Idalia asked. Her smile indicated she was holding back laughter.

"Nay," she argued, turning for her sister to tie the side of her kirtle. "After I stumbled into my room after being thoroughly dismissed by Terric, I fancied a bit of rest. I only lay down for a moment."

She did not elaborate on her feelings about his dismissal.

Idalia snorted. "A moment. Do you remember me helping you out of your gown?"

She declined to answer.

"Much has happened since then, but perhaps you should eat before we discuss it."

Roysa did not like her sister's tone. The humor had all leaked out of her voice. Something was seriously amiss. She spun around as soon as Idalia finished tying the fabric of her gown.

"Talk about what?"

Finished, Idalia stood back, averting her eyes. Aye, something was definitely wrong.

"Battle. Dromsley is preparing for battle."

CHAPTER 11

T erric was exhausted.

He'd hardly slept the night before, but he dismissed the thought of his bed waiting in the adjoining chamber. All he could think about was John's next move. Though he, Gilbert, and Lance had spent the last two days going over the plans for a possible battle or siege, ever since Roysa delivered her alarming news about Ulster, he decided he would look at them again.

His people depended on his readiness for battle. He would fulfill his obligations to them just as his father had taught him.

Grabbing the tankard, Terric poured himself an ale and moved toward the fireplace. It was the largest one he'd ever seen, its hearth spanning most of the thick eastern wall. They'd spent little time here growing up, but he still had a clear image of his father standing in this very spot, looking at the flames of the fire. That had been the night he and Rory had asked their mother to accompany Father to the tournament so they all might go. He couldn't recall his sister Cait being there, but she must have been nearby.

If she'd said no, how different his life might have been.

Best not to think of that.

Or of Roysa.

A distraction was the one thing he absolutely could not afford. It was part of the reason he'd barely left his solar these last two days, opting instead to take his meals there. This evening, however, he'd found himself wavering. He'd nearly decided to take his dinner in the hall.

Because he wished to see her.

Nay, he wished to ravish her.

It was foolish. Beyond foolish. Too many people depended on him for him to give in to his own desires.

He barely heard it at first, but the sound was more distinct when it repeated itself. Terric moved toward the door. Aye, it was a knock. Perhaps Lance or Gilbert suffered from the same sleeplessness.

"I guess I am not the only one . . ."

He froze as he opened the door.

Not Lance. Or his marshal.

A very confused Lady Roysa stood there, eyes wide. And his body immediately responded. She wore a long velvet robe, as fine as one of her fancy gowns. The garment was not exactly revealing, but it was intimate. Given the time of night, he imagined it covered only a shift.

By the blood of Christ.

"I was looking for Idalia. I was sure her bedchamber was here, the second door past the stairwell. Is she . . ."

"Is she inside?" he finished for her. "Nay, my lady. You have the correct door, but the wrong floor." He pointed below them. "She and Lance are just below us."

When she began to move away, he discovered he did not yet wish for her to leave.

"Did she—" he started and Roysa stopped to look at him, her lips slightly parted.

Terric continued to stare. Her hair had always been pulled away from her face, but now it hung loose around her shoulders, a shock of darkness against pale cream. The single candle she held gave her an almost ethereal glow. She looked vulnerable almost.

Those parted lips, not intended as an invitation. But damned if he didn't want to take it as one.

So very different than the woman he'd met in the front of the gatehouse that first night.

"Did Idalia explain?"

A flash of fiery defiance crossed her gaze. "Aye. Though if you had offered a quick explanation, it would have avoided much confusion. Such as, 'Ulster? Why, he is one of John's staunchest supporters, a strategist that should not be this far north. He is likely colluding with Langham to attack.'"

She was asking for courtesy. But they were at war, or near enough—courtesy did not warrant his attention.

"I needed to prepare my men."

"Understood, my lord. It would have been a waste of your time to spend a moment explaining the circumstances to a mere woman. I apologize for disturbing you."

She made to leave again.

Terric's hand shot out to stop her. Her wrist was so small, his fingers wrapped around it easily. He forced himself to drop it, but he could not force himself to send her away.

But neither should she stay.

Still he heard himself say, "Do not leave."

If he were truthful with himself, he'd wanted to see her all day. He'd woken up in the dead of night thinking of her. And now that she was here, he did not want her to go. He nodded inside. "A tankard of ale before you sleep?"

She hesitated, with good reason. It was hardly proper for her to share a drink with him in his solar in the middle of the night. Unchaperoned.

But this was not just any woman. She was Idalia's sister. Lance's sister-in-law, which almost made her family.

He nearly laughed at the thought. Roysa was not Idalia, and his cock knew the difference. It would not be fooled so easily.

She met his gaze, her eyes searching for answers. He knew she wouldn't find any—for he didn't understand himself any better than she did.

"Perhaps just one," she said.

Terric knew what desire looked like. He'd seen those hooded eyes, those parted lips on other women, but never had such a look made him react like this. The jolt of lust he felt was too powerful—so much so it nearly made him change his mind. Roysa was not one to trifle with. Idalia would rightly kill him were he to seduce her sister. A woman who'd recently lost her husband. A woman he had no intention of marrying.

But one did not tryst with a woman such as Roysa. A pity, but a fact as well.

"You are certain?" he forced himself to ask. His throat nearly closed on itself for the thickness of his voice.

"Aye. I am sure."

No four words had ever held such promise.

Such damnation, he corrected.

CHAPTER 12

R oysa stepped inside.

Heart hammering in her chest, she listened to the door closing behind her, a bar-
rier that had just been breached. A line that had just
been crossed.

He must have felt it too. Was it possible Roysa
was alone in this?

When Terric came from around her and stepped
back into view, she knew the answer.

Towering over her in nothing more than trewes
and an undertunic, the Earl of Dromsley, the chief of
Clan Kennaugh, looked at her as a starving man
might regard a banquet. No other man had ever given
her such a look. She discounted the suitors who'd visited throughout the years. And did not even consider
the man she had married. She'd learned, very quickly,
Walter had only ever seen her as Lord Stanton's eldest
daughter. A prize to be won. If she had convinced
herself otherwise in the beginning, it was only because that's what she had so desperately wanted.

Just as she desperately wanted Terric to kiss her.

In truth, despite her ire with him, despite the
danger they were all in, she'd thought of nothing else
these past days.

"Ale," he said, more a comment than a question.

She nodded, not sure what else to do.

When he turned from her, Roysa let out a breath. Was she really standing here, in nothing but her shift and a robe, in Terric's solar chamber?

She watched as he filled a second tankard from the carafe on the table.

Like her father's solar, this one had been prepared to receive visitors. The lord's solar was a common meeting place, especially in the winter. It was nearly always the warmest chamber in the castle, its walls so covered in tapestries one could barely see the stone behind them.

This one was no exception.

The fireplace was overly large, almost ominous.

Much like the man standing before it.

He wordlessly handed her the tankard. What could either of them say? This was wildly inappropriate. They'd only just made up. She'd been recently widowed. He had a battle or siege to prepare for.

"I thought, at first, you resembled your sister. But there is something very different about you as well."

His suggestive tone was not what she'd been expecting.

"Some would disagree."

When he walked toward the chairs arranged in front of the fire, Roysa followed. She sat opposite him, clutching the pewter tankard between both hands. Engraved with roses climbing up from the bottom, it felt as cold as the fire was warm.

"My father brought them from Scotland."

She looked up.

"He enjoyed having something in nearly every room"—he pointed to the tapestry just behind where she sat—"that reminded him of Scotland."

She knew so little of his family.

"Tell me of him."

Even if she hadn't known his father was no longer with them, Terric's expression would have given the fact away.

"There was no man, or woman, alive who could offer a bad word about my father. He loved our family nearly as much as he did our clan."

She cocked her head to the side. "Should it not be just the opposite?"

Terric took a sip of ale. "Not for the chief."

"Not for you," she clarified.

"Nay."

"You never married." She blurted that without thinking.

"I did. My wife is back home, waiting patiently for me to return from England."

Her mouth dropped. "But . . . you are . . ."

He was married?

It took her a moment to realize Terric had been teasing. By then, it was too late. Her reaction had been telling, indeed.

So was the fact that she'd come here alone.

"I could not resist."

"It was just unexpected. You do not seem the kind of man to tease."

She took a sip, a long one, wishing it were wine but glad to have something to do with her hands.

"What kind of man do you suppose I am, Lady Roysa?"

His tone did not match his easy smile. Roysa thought carefully before answering.

"Although you are not quite as serious in disposition as my brother-in-law, I can tell your duty weighs on you. You remind me of my father, who wakes early each morn to serve Stanton and lies down each night wondering what else he might have done. You're not arrogant, as I first believed, but you are more confident than most. And loyal. I know that from what

Idalia told me last eve. Of the order. Of how you met."

He simply stared at her, his smile slipping away. She didn't blame him.

The story was a brutal one—the kind that forges a bond to last a lifetime. Terric had met Lance and the other members of the order, Conrad and Guy, at the Tournament of the North when they were but boys. They'd come upon his sister, Cait, while she was being attacked by one of the king's guard. The man had pushed her down onto the riverbank and hiked her gown to her waist. If they'd come along a few moments later, he would have raped her.

She knew little of the details, but somehow the four young boys had overpowered the king's guard, a well-trained knight, and killed him in the ensuing scuffle. Fearing retribution, they'd dumped his body in the nearby river, keeping only the hilt of his broken sword as a reminder of the horrific event.

Hence the Order of the Broken Blade.

According to Idalia, Conrad was the only one of them to bear a physical scar, on his cheek, but Roysa imagined all of them carried the event with them. Terric and his sister most of all.

Idalia had also told her that Terric blamed himself for not being able to protect his sister. He'd been the smallest of the four at the time, and he'd been knocked to the ground first.

And relentless. She thought of Idalia's story. Relentless in his pursuit to become stronger than any others.

He was no longer smiling.

Roysa hadn't meant to dampen the mood between them, but she was curious about her host, curious also about the event that had brought the four men of the Order of the Broken Blade together.

"Did you know the others before"—she stumbled on her words—"before it happened?"

Instead of taking offense to her question, Terric leaned back further in his seat, crossing his legs in front of him. "I knew Conrad, but not well. Cait actually met him first."

"Your sister."

"Aye, she is just a year older than I am. She was much too young that day."

His tone sounded relaxed almost, but his expression was anything but.

"I do not say this because she is my sister, but a sweeter woman could not be found in Scotland. The opinion is not mine alone—all who have met her think the same. Cait is kind, mayhap too much so."

"'Tis possible to be too kind?"

"Aye." He did not hesitate. "When the bastard approached her, Cait had an uneasy feeling. She knew it was wrong for her to be there alone, by the riverbank. She'd taken a walk, you see, and ventured too far from the tents. It was her first tournament."

The Tournament of the North was also the first one Roysa had attended. She'd found it quite overwhelming, really. It was like the busiest marketplace imaginable stuck in the midst of a battle. The place teemed with activity from sunup to sundown.

She could imagine easily wanting a moment of respite.

"Conrad and I went looking for her. Lance and Guy came upon the scene at nearly the same time we did. They were strangers to us, as they were to Cait, but they did not hesitate." His jaw clenched. "They did not hesitate. The four of us attacked a fully trained knight with the type of vengeance that could only be wrought from boys of ten and four knowing they are severely disadvantaged."

Terric stood abruptly. He took his time filling his

tankard, and she felt sure he was seeking a respite from the horrible memory. When he sat back down, his hands no longer clenched the poor tankard as if he were attempting to choke the life out of it.

She attempted to shift the tone of their discussion.

"What kind of woman do you suppose I am?" she asked, mimicking his earlier words.

It worked. Terric's slow smile did something to her insides. But he was no longer angry, at least.

"When I first met you, I thought you the worst sort of woman, if I am speaking truly."

Though she'd sensed as much, his words still stung.

"The kind of woman who cares about her appearance, but not to impress others, as I first believed. In truth, I loved such a woman, who later became enamored with my brother when she realized it was possible he would someday be chief."

The fleeting stab of pain at Terric's admission he had loved a woman scared her.

"Become chief? 'Tis such a thing possible?"

And why? Though she kept that question to herself.

"It seems unlikely at the moment, but if he matures," Terric shrugged. "In order to properly care for our clan, and the people of Dromsley . . ." He stopped. "But we were speaking of you."

Terric leaned forward, "And why you sought to impress your father."

She sucked in a breath.

"At least, 'tis why, I believe, you concerned yourself with your looks at first. Now it has become a habit. You play the role of a dutiful daughter, the sort of woman who will one day manage a castle of her own, and you do it quite capably."

His words were painfully accurate, so much so Roysa suddenly regretted asking the question.

"You are also devoted to your family. A quality I can admire. You are fierce and self-contained and have no need to seek the opinion of those around you."

Roysa tried not to let him see how the words affected her.

"You are the sort who is so beautiful others almost fear speaking to her."

He believes me beautiful.

She hid her embarrassment at the compliment behind the tankard, sipping slowly and trying to untangle his words.

"Have I missed the mark, my lady?"

When he stood, Roysa thought she might faint. She'd never done so before in her life, and this would be a poor time to start. The fire she'd thought made the chamber quite comfortable now seemed stifling.

Too soon, he stood at the foot of her seat. And held out his hand.

CHAPTER 13

Terric had made many bad decisions in his life.

Allowing Rory too much control as his second before he was ready.

Not moving against King John sooner.

But this? Kissing the sister of his friend? It was a poor idea, indeed, and Terric knew it down to his bones. He'd known it before he'd invited her inside.

But he extended his hand anyway, merely because he wanted to. He wanted her.

She looked at it a moment, Roysa's expressive eyes not failing her now. Despite all the reasons she shouldn't take it, she clearly wanted to.

And so she did.

Her hand felt so small and soft in his much larger palm. A perfect fit, really.

He took the tankard from her other hand and leaned down to place it on a nearby table. He'd never admit it, of course, but he was nervous. It had been some time since he'd kissed a woman.

Unlike his brother, Terric did not dally with the servants. Since coming to England, he had been focused on their cause and not much else.

And Roysa was no ordinary woman.

Releasing her hand, Terric slid his hands up either side of her neck, his fingers quickly becoming entangled in hair so soft he groaned before thinking better of it. He considered warning her of the dangers of what they were about to do, but it was clear she already knew.

They were two unmarried adults who desired each other, and nothing else much mattered at the moment. When he leaned forward, their lips finally touching, Terric tightened his grip on her head, pulling her even closer.

When she opened her mouth for him, Terric took full advantage. He moved much more quickly than intended, his tongue finding hers and tangling with it as if they had done this before. He kissed her as if he'd wanted to do it from the moment they'd met. And perhaps he had.

When her arms moved to his back, Terric finally acknowledged to himself that the simple kiss had become anything but.

He tore his mouth from hers, knowing two things.

That kiss could make him forget all else that was important to him.

And he did not care.

"You've not kissed that way before?"

She'd known to open for him, but from there it had been as hesitant as a virgin's kiss.

"Nay."

They were close enough for Terric to smell the combination of ale and mint on her breath. Too close for them to carry on a conversation without him succumbing to temptation. He moved back slightly but kept his hands locked around her head, unwilling for her to move too far from him.

"How is that possible?"

She had the fullest lips he'd ever seen. Lips made

to be kissed.

"My husband was . . ." She blinked.

"He kissed you, surely."

Roysa nodded. "But not in that way, precisely."

He could see she was embarrassed, but Terric wanted to understand.

"Did he abuse you, Roysa?"

Please do not say aye.

"He did not abuse me. But neither did he kiss me that way. As if . . . as if he cared for my pleasure."

Terric understood, although he would have gladly pummeled Stokesay, were he not dead. The man had been a blind fool.

"I do not mean for you to be embarrassed."

"I am not," she lied.

"Aye," he disagreed. "You are, but should not be. There is nothing more natural than this." He pulled her back toward him. "You say he did not care for your pleasure when he kissed you . . ."

"Or at any time. He came to me rarely and always after drinking heavily."

To beget an heir.

Not unusual in an arranged marriage, but very much so when the woman looked like Roysa. Even now the thought of his hands on her bare skin was enough to make Terric forget they were preparing for a possible battle. A fight for his home, for his life . . . for vengeance.

"Enough talk of him," he whispered, lowering his head again. "I will do what he did not. I will show you pleasure, Roysa."

He kissed just under her ear, holding her hair back and taking advantage of the long swathe of neck he'd revealed.

"Starting here."

This time, he used his tongue. Little by little, he teased his way from her neck toward her cheek.

When he'd just reached her lips, he stopped. Heart racing, cock pulsing, he did nothing. When she opened her mouth, presumably to ask why he had stopped, Terric held nothing back.

He kissed her, hard.

Tilting her head with his hands, Terric showed Roysa everything a kiss could and should be. This was no gentle lesson. He wondered if she could feel the evidence of his need pressed against her. It would be such a simple thing to part the heavy material of her robe, let it fall to the ground between them and continue his exploration of her luscious body.

Especially when she made that sound. It was his undoing.

But through the haze of lust, Terric felt the certainty it would lead to more than a few simple touches. Still, he could not help but reach inside her robe to find a perfectly shaped breast. He lifted it, rubbed his thumb across her nipple, and nearly came in his trewes when he found it already hard, as if awaiting his touch.

Congratulating himself for being an even better man than he'd thought his parents had raised, Terric stopped. He stepped away.

His hands felt empty, as they did every time he handed his sword off to a squire. As if a part of him were missing.

"I did not intend to do that—" He stopped, recognizing the lie, and told her an unshakable truth. "That was going to lead down a path neither of us is ready for."

He dared her to disagree. And was disappointed when she didn't.

"Aye. 'Tis unseemly for me, so recently widowed."

Terric had not meant that at all. "Nay, Roysa. Being widowed by a man like that is a blessing, not a cause for mourning."

But she felt guilty even so. He saw it on her face.

"I only meant"—he frowned—"I would very much enjoy showing you *all* of the pleasures of the flesh. Not just the ones that come from kissing."

Endearingly, she blushed at the word.

He would incite that blush for a more tantalizing reason next time.

There should not be a next time, you fool.

"And it might be hard to explain to Idalia and Lance why we should find ourselves alone, unchaperoned, in my bedchamber."

She did not flinch. "Is such an explanation necessary?"

Oh God, no. Do not, Roysa. I am not strong enough.

"I am no virgin."

"And I am no saint. But you do not understand."

Roysa's chest rose and fell, the tantalizing sight calling to him like a siren's song.

"I believe I do. You are not prepared to take a wife."

He winced. "My duty is to my family. To my clan. The people of Dromsley. And to the order."

She frowned. "And to England, no? Is that not the battle cry of the order? To save your country from a tyrant's rule?"

Terric shook his head. "Nay. It is Conrad's goal. One that's shared by Lance and Guy, and all the men who signed their names to the document that declared them traitors."

"But not yours?"

Terric was, if anything, aware of his flaws. And this was certainly the biggest of them all.

"Nay, not mine. My only other duty is to vengeance."

He silently thanked her for the reminder.

"Which is why this"—he motioned between them—"cannot be."

CHAPTER 14

"Tell me," Idalia insisted.

Roysa and her sister watched from the parapets as preparations were made. Just a few days earlier, there had been little activity in either the inner or outer ward. Getting from one place to another had been a chore due to the snow.

That had changed. The men were moving with purpose; she and her sister were the sole exceptions. Both of them had wanted a bit of air, despite the cold, although Roysa now regretted that she'd come out here with Idalia. It made her sister's questions more difficult to escape. She'd begun her inquiries earlier, at breakfast, and hadn't stopped.

"There is naught to tell. I am tired. Worried, of course. The reason should be evident."

They had a clear view of the training yard.

"You are not yourself."

Nay, she was not.

Roysa looked at her sister, head hooded, cheeks pinkened with the cold. She looked younger than normal. As if they were girls still. If only the problems that had seemed so monumental to them then—getting out of lessons early and being shooed away from the kitchens by their mother—were their only worries now.

"He kissed me," she blurted.

Idalia clearly did not understand. "He . . ."

She waited for Idalia to realize who she spoke of, and it struck her that her sister did not look well pleased. Well, that made two of them. Roysa was not very pleased with herself either.

"I did not realize . . . well, of course Terric is a very handsome man. And you sat together in the hall for quite a while the other day. But . . ."

Roysa had to laugh at Idalia's expression. She looked . . . scandalized.

"I know," she conceded. "I am so recently widowed—"

"By a man who had sexual relations with his sister-in-law? Who was very likely murdered by his own brother? Do you really believe you should be mourning such a man?"

Nay, Roysa did not. "Then why are you so displeased?"

Idalia did not attempt to deny it. Instead, she said, "I've gotten to know Terric quite well over the last several months."

The idea that Idalia might tell her something terrible about Terric . . .

Please do not.

He'd told her they could not be, which she understood, but she could not shake the lure of what he'd said before that, about showing her pleasure. She'd thought of that all night long, tossing and turning as she did so.

She wanted to know such pleasure.

"He is a hard man," Idalia said at last.

Roysa knew it well.

"I like him, of course. Lance thinks of him as a brother. But . . ."

Idalia looked at her with such a look of pity, she wished she had held her tongue about the kiss.

"He is like Father in some ways."

"In many ways," she agreed.

"He is not a man I could imagine for a husband." The words were said gently, as if Idalia believed she were dissuading her from a dear wish.

Roysa's shoulders sagged in relief. "That is all?"

"He is very focused on this mission," Idalia said, furrowing her brow. "It would surprise me greatly if he took a wife."

Roysa waited, her lips pursed together.

"Though you are wonderful, of course. Any man should be as lucky to have a wife such as you."

She attempted to keep her expression serious.

"Especially when you are being kind. Not that you are not always kind, but at times I wish you would be easier on yourself. That you would not expect such perfection . . . Roysa? Are you laughing at me?"

"Nay," she said, doing just that. "I would never do so." She shook her head. "Not at all. Never."

Except that she was.

And finally, her little sister understood.

"You don't want Terric for a husband."

The very word terrified her. Though maybe slightly less than before the previous evening. "Nay. I have had one and would not care to repeat such an arrangement again."

"But you said . . ."

"You are married, Idalia. To a man who loves you. Surely you can understand a woman might want something else from a man?"

"You don't want to marry him. You want to have sex with him?"

Or at least be introduced to the pleasures he'd promised. Roysa was about to respond when a voice interrupted them from behind.

"Have sex with whom?"

❧

"YOU COULD NOT BE MORE OUTRAGEOUS," TERRIC declared, watching the men from the sidelines with his arms folded over his chest. He always trained alongside his men. But not today. This was no longer training but preparing for battle. Or perhaps a siege. He alternated between encouraging the men, speaking to his marshal, and sneering at his friend. Lance had seen his wife atop the parapets and left them for the sole purpose of stealing a kiss.

He'd have gladly followed and done the same, the mere sight of Roysa stirring him quite easily.

"I was not gone long," Lance objected.

"That hardly matters. I dare you to repeat those words to Guy or Conrad. 'I will be back soon. I need to kiss my wife.' Who says such a thing?"

Terric's eyes tracked Gilbert as the marshal walked between the men, shouting orders though never berating anyone. He was a capable marshal, and he was lucky to have such a man.

"I'm not ashamed of wanting to kiss my wife. Besides, Guy would understand well enough. Though I'd never have believed it, the man's heart actually beats inside his chest."

Terric laughed at that. None of them had ever believed Guy, a mercenary, would marry. But the rest of them had agreed that he seemed happier with Sabine than he'd ever been before.

"Even Conrad understands the notion of being in love."

"I understand it. I just do not wish to partake in it." He turned toward Lance. "Besides, when has Conrad ever been in love?"

Lance just gave him a private smile, a look that

said he knew something but did not wish to share. Could it be a secret about Conrad?

"Out with it, Lance."

His friend just shrugged. "You chastised me for kissing my wife, but it seems you've taken the time out of our preparation for battle to do the same. Though not with my wife, of course," he rushed to add.

Terric groaned. He'd assumed Lance would find out eventually—it stood to reason Roysa would tell her sister, who would in turn tell Lance—but he'd hoped it might not be so soon.

"There's naught to tell. It was one kiss. That should not have happened. And will not happen again."

If Lance had looked pleased before, he now appeared as if he had just been crowned tournament champion. He knew something else, something he wasn't saying.

"Your loyalty is to the order above all," Terric said. "Even your wife."

Lance chuckled.

"I do not remember that in the oath we took." His smiled fled. "Either time."

Terric did not wish to talk of that first occasion, although it seemed many of their conversations ended up touching upon their initial meeting.

"We said it," he nodded, firm. "I remember that part clearly."

"I don't believe we did."

"You will tell me what you know."

"I don't believe I will."

"Lancelin."

He *hated* his given name, but he merely scowled at the mention of it. It was clear he did not intend to reveal his information. Frustrated though not terribly surprised, Terric turned to glance at Gilbert—

and saw his marshal was pointing toward the North Gate.

Terric squinted.

"Who is it?" Lance asked.

He could not tell yet. But the man's face slowly came into view. And from the newcomer's quickening pace, Terric knew the news was not good.

CHAPTER 15

His scout had returned from The Wild Boar, an inn that some called the most strategic location along the border. Every rumor from England or Scotland, whether it be from the north or the south, eventually made its way to the Boar.

And there were whispers of the king's supporters mobilizing against them. Paired with the information Roysa had brought them, it seemed to indicate the rumors were true.

King John did not intend to make good on his agreement to meet with them. He planned to attack.

Now, if only his men could settle on a strategy. Although they'd been discussing the matter for days, they were still at a standoff. His captain thought they should prepare for a siege only if Ulster marched against them; his marshal thought they'd best do so anyway.

These men had been entrusted to keep Dromsley Castle safe in his absence. In his father's absence. He respected them and understood their hesitation.

Even so, they were wrong.

If John effectively mobilized Ulster, the order's mission would begin to crumble. Dromsley was as well positioned as any fortification to withstand a siege. They were well supplied and as prepared as possible. It would last for months.

Although Terric should not have allowed Rory to delay sending the men. Indeed, he'd made a grave mistake in doing so—he knew they could not afford to wait. If the rumors proved true, Dromsley would be under attack the moment the weather broke.

They could not bend lest they break.

"We fight," he announced over the others' arguing in his solar. He moved away from the table, his decision made.

"Tomorrow we will plan, though you have my leave to prepare for siege as well," he said. "Tonight, we eat." Something they had not done all day.

The marshal and captain did not know him well—before this winter he'd only visited Dromsley on occasion—but Lance had been his friend, his brother in the order for years. He was the only one who did not question his decision or attempt to dissuade him. Lance knew he did not waver once he'd made a decision.

It was done. They would fight.

But he really did need to eat. Tomorrow was soon enough for them to continue their planning.

"My lord?" Gilbert grimaced.

They doubted him, and to succeed, he would need their confidence and support. His father's face flashed before him. His words rang in Terric's ears.

If you believe, they will too.

"If Ulster and Langham combined forces, we will undoubtedly be outmanned—you are correct about that. But not outmaneuvered. If victory were not within our grasp, I'd not sacrifice Dromsley's men unnecessarily."

Whether it was his tone or his words that put Gilbert at ease, Terric couldn't be sure. Although he was still not pleased, Gilbert looked slightly reassured

as he glanced down at the hand-drawn map of Dromsley and its surrounding lands they'd been studying.

"We will need to discuss a battleground."

"Aye," he said.

"And take a full accounting of their combined
men."

Terric agreed again.

Still, despite his extreme hunger, Terric waited.
He wished to have his marshal's full cooperation and
confidence.

"We should speak to the men as soon as possible,"
Gilbert continued.

He paused, wanting his marshal to know he understood the gravity of the decision he'd made. "I
agree," he said finally.

Satisfied for now, Gilbert gestured toward the
door Terric desperately wanted to exit. Because he
was hungry.

Not because he wanted to see Roysa.

"Your gown . . ."

Roysa ignored her sister's shocked expression and
the grin that followed, pretending it meant nothing.
After what Lance had overheard, and the giggling
that had ensued because of it, she could not deny the
reason for this particular choice of dress.

"The maid is quite capable. She's aired out all five
of the ones I brought and even repaired the hem on
one."

"Only five?"

Roysa had been happy to see her sister at the
door, asking if she wanted to walk down to the hall
together for the evening meal. Maybe she should not
have been so quick in her joy.

"I was advised to bring little. Or take nothing."

They navigated the dark corridors with the aid of two candles, the scant light flickering against the walls as they walked.

"I hate him."

Roysa slowed. Idalia never hated anyone. Not even the boy who'd tossed mud at her face when she was nine. It was preposterous for him to have done such a thing, to the lord's daughter no less, but Idalia, in her typical way, had wiped it off and continued on to the market as if nothing had happened.

Roysa had always wished she could be more like her sister in many ways.

"I am not fond of him either," she admitted. "Apparently Walter felt the same way."

Idalia burst out laughing, and it was all Roysa could do not to join her. It had been an incredibly uncharitable thing to say. The man was dead. But she so wanted to be rid of the guilt that threatened to strangle her.

Besides, why should she spare a kind thought for a man who had mistreated her? For his brother, who likely wanted her dead?

But surely a good person would, wouldn't they?

"Am I flawed?" she blurted.

It took a moment for Idalia to stop laughing, as if she did not at first realize it were a serious question. When she did stop, it was abrupt.

"Oh Roysa, whatever do you mean?" she said.

She wished she could take the words back.

"I cannot decide if I care for others too much, or too little. If I should be more like Father, or you."

Two people she admired deeply, who were as different as can be.

"You've never asked such a question before."

Roysa wished she hadn't done so now. Her tongue had run way with her.

"You are my sister. Always dressed"—she gestured

with her free hand toward Roysa's gown—"to perfection. Father's favorite. I do not begrudge it," she rushed to add. "And neither does Tilly. Not"—she smiled—"that we understand it. Father can be . . ."

"Difficult," Roysa finished for her.

"Aye. Tilly and I have always wanted to be more like *you*, not Father."

Roysa did not want to disappoint her sister, but neither could she mislead her.

"I am far from perfect," she confessed.

But Idalia did not react as she would have expected.

"Of course you're not perfect. And as for who you should strive to be more like, the answer is evident."

Roysa knew it too. Who would strive to emulate a man like her father when the very essence of a good, kind person stood before her?

"You should be more like you."

That was hardly the answer she'd expected.

"But I am—"

"Exactly as you should be. Rail against a dead man, if it pleases you. Empathize with him, even after he wronged you, if it allows you to heal. Neither is wrong. 'Tis only wrong to chastise yourself for being honest about your feelings."

"When did you become so wise?"

She meant the question sincerely. This was a different woman than the younger sister she'd left behind in Stanton. Meeting Lance, and supporting his work with the order, had changed her.

And maybe Terric could be a part of her own journey?

Nay. He has made his intentions clear. Best listen to them.

"I'm no wiser than you. Indeed, I'm shocked you're still standing on both feet given everything you've been through. You lost your husband and were

85

forced out of your home, only to flee to safety in what is soon to become a battleground."

Roysa did smile then. "You forgot to add that I was kissed by the handsomest of men."

Idalia cocked her head to the side. "Do you really think so? He is much too large, I think. And his nose . . ."

"Is perfect! There is nothing wrong with Terric's . . ."

Idalia had already started walking. Roysa followed the sound of her laughter toward the hall.

Thankfully, there was little chance the man with a perfect nose would be in attendance. Her father's war councils sometimes lasted for days, and Terric had made himself scarce these past few days. She wouldn't make the mistake of stumbling into his solar again, so they were unlikely to see each other.

Then why are you wearing this gown?

Roysa pushed away the pesky thought.

CHAPTER 16

Her heart sped up as she stepped into the hall.
He was there.

Sitting exactly where he would be had an impending battle not demanded his attention. Perhaps he was not so much like her father after all.

Terric and Lance stood as they entered the room. The hall seemed to grow quiet, which did nothing to quell Roysa's growing sense of doom. Nothing good could come of this attraction. Idalia had warned her away, and she would do best to heed her sister's warning.

And yet . . .

There was no denying she'd decided to wear her favorite lilac gown tonight in the hopes he'd see it. Made of Italian silk, it had been a somewhat extravagant purchase—a gift from her mother for her wedding.

The gown was a single color, from its long split sleeves to the embroidery winding its way from her shoulders down the center of the dress to the low vee that hit below her waist. Cut just above the elbows, the sleeves' slits allowed for the fabric to hang well below her hands. When lifted, her arms peeked out easily. When lowered, they were completely hidden.

The gown had been meant for her wedding.

Roysa had decided not to wear it the morn of the wedding. It had felt . . . wrong. She hadn't precisely understood why, but that feeling of wrongness had been strong enough that she'd risked upsetting her mother by changing their plan. Now, with the benefit of hindsight, she understood part of her had, even then, understood the marriage was a mistake.

She'd taken the dress with her to Stokesay, but she'd never worn it.

Until tonight.

"He's staring," Idalia whispered.

Roysa did not need to be told. Her eyes had locked with his as soon as she stepped into the room. Looking at him, she could not help but remember the feel of those lips moving against hers, that hand on her flesh. In truth, she hadn't stopped thinking of either since the night before.

"Lady Roysa. My beautiful wife," Lance greeted them.

At first, Roysa had thought her sister's blacksmith a touch too dour, but the man did know how to smile, she'd learned—he just did it so rarely, each smile felt like a gift. He was the husband her sister needed, and she loved him for it.

"Lord Tuleen," she said with a nod, acknowledging his status as the new lord of Tuleen Castle, even though he and his new wife had not yet taken up residence there.

As she approached the table, she took note of the table setting. Her seat had been moved to Terric's left, with Lance and Idalia to his right. She wasn't the only one to notice.

"I would speak to you this eve," Terric said, watching her. "But if you'd prefer to sit next to Idalia, I understand."

It was no simple thing, the placement of guests.

The most important people in attendance at a meal sat next to the lord. She knew it. Lance and Idalia knew it. Even those seated below them, looking up at the dais, knew it. Their stares were so pointed, she felt them.

Was she reading too much into Terric's gesture?

Rather than respond to him, she simply moved to the side of the high-backed chair and sat. Terric had waved away the servant who should have assisted her and pushed in her seat himself.

She smiled into the hall, at no one in particular. Just as she'd thought, most everyone was staring. Finally, after what seemed like a very long time indeed, the hundred or so men, some with their wives and others alone, turned back to their first course.

"Surely they think it odd a stranger is seated next to you?"

Roysa looked at him head-on.

And wished she hadn't.

Terric made no attempt to hide the desire in his eyes. And her body made no attempt to temper its reaction. Warmth flooded her, a joy that extended from her feet up to the very top of her head.

"They know you are the sister of my honored guest."

"Who should be seated next to that same sister," she countered.

They stopped conversing when a girl, no more than eight and ten, poured each of them wine from the pitcher that had sat in front of them. When she caught the girl's eyes, Roysa was surprised to see unhappiness there. Had she offended her in some way?

"Conventions are not so stringent where I'm from. None would think it odd for you to be seated next to me."

Where I'm from. For a moment, she'd forgotten he was, in fact, a Scot. Because his family lived just over the border, his dress was not so different, his accent barely detectable. But Terric was not an Englishman.

"Do you miss your home?"

Terric didn't answer at first. Instead, he smiled at the maid as she placed a bowl of soup in front of him. The look the young girl gave him, which could only be described as besotted, made Roysa realize why the girl had seemed so upset with her. She liked Terric. As did everyone, it seemed.

"Aye. Being away from Bradon Moor for this long is the most difficult thing I've ever done," he said when the maid finally walked away. "Though my brother has taken my place, we don't always agree on matters. And the people here hardly know me, even though I've been visiting since I was a boy. But someday, this may well be my home in truth."

"When your brother is ready to take your place."

"Aye."

"How did your parents meet?"

She sipped her wine, content to listen to Terric talk.

"The same way we did." He nodded to Lance. "At the Tournament of the North. Although the circumstances were very different. She quite literally fell on top of him when a horse shied too close. He caught her, and apparently never let go."

"Did her parents care she'd fallen for a Scotsman?"

"Would yours?"

Though she understood his meaning, Roysa could not help but blush at the idea of telling her father she planned to marry a Scots clan chief.

"Perhaps. Though less so if he were also an English earl."

"Fortunately, it did not take long for my grandfather to accept my father. His unwavering support of him against King Henry's machinations helped."

"So you hated both father and son?" she asked, though it was a silly question.

"Aye. King Henry wronged my mother. And his man, a very close advisor, assaulted my sister. What kind of king allows such a man to serve him? And the son is obviously no better than his father. His cruelties became apparent nearly the moment his reign began. 'Tis what happens when power goes unchecked."

"But there have been many good kings who have not abused their power."

"And too many bad ones who have. A king is nothing but a man with a crown. There are good and bad men, and women, and they do not typically become any nobler for having power over the lives of those beneath them."

Indeed. The same could be said of Walter, she thought.

Terric spoke calmly, but the tic in his jaw gave him away. Though Roysa did not blame him for his anger. She understood it, maybe even appreciated it.

"What of your parents?" he asked, deliberately changing the subject.

Roysa hadn't yet touched her own soup. Instead, she watched as Terric ate, ignoring the way Idalia and Lance kept glancing over at them.

"They met on their wedding day."

Not an unusual occurrence here, but perhaps it was more so in Scotland. Terric seemed surprised.

"It was arranged, of course," she said.

"Of course."

"And more difficult for my mother, I believe, than my father."

She peered around Terric and Lance to look at her sister. Idalia did not know of their mother's past, and she'd not learn it from her. It was not her tale to tell.

Her sister leaned forward. "You're speaking of Mother's first marriage, are you not?"

So Mother had told her too. She'd shared the story with Roysa after Walter's first visit. At the time, Roysa had thought her mother was being supportive of her love match—but now she wondered if she'd hoped to show Roysa that the affection she'd built up in her mind was naught but a wish. A dream.

It was not the kind of love to hang a marriage on.

"When did she tell you?"

Idalia exchanged a glance with her husband. "When she realized I was falling in love with a blacksmith."

Terric drummed his fingers on the stem of his goblet. "It appears I'm the only one who doesn't know the story."

All too aware of her warming cheeks, Roysa explained, "She was supposed to marry my father, but she fell in love with a Scottish reiver. They married in secret, but of course my grandfather eventually learned of it. He never accepted her husband, even though they had . . ."

She looked to Idalia for help, but her sister did not seem inclined to finish her sentence. Indeed, she was grinning in a most unhelpful manner.

"Relations," she finished lamely.

"Ahhh," Terric said, his eyes twinkling in amusement as they met hers. "She was no longer a virgin."

Roysa dearly wished she'd not taken a sip of wine to hide her embarrassment. Nearly spitting it out, she glared at Terric. The man knew he was mortifying her.

"Just so."

Roysa sat up in her seat.

"Tragically, he died less than a year after their wedding. My father apparently knew of it, but he still wished to marry her."

"Knew that she'd been married," Terric asked, "or that his intended was no longer a virgin?"

Lance swatted his friend, and Roysa silently thanked him.

"You are a brute," she said.

"I am," Terric agreed good-naturedly. "'Tis quite a tale."

Thankful for the bowl of pottage stew in front of her, she gave it her full attention.

"Almost as fantastical as the story of a lord's daughter falling in love with a blacksmith," he said, a smile in his voice.

Or of the lady's other daughter falling for a Scotsman after being cast out by her dead husband's brother.

Quite a tale, indeed. If she were falling for said Scotsman.

Which she most certainly was not.

CHAPTER 17

The last time Terric had laughed this hard, his brother had fallen from the loft inside their stables at Bradon Moor. Some might call him uncharitable to laugh at such a thing, but Rory had been seducing the stablemaster's daughter at the time—and Terric had entered the stables with the girl's father. He'd tumbled to the ground while hurriedly attempting to don his trewes.

Their parents had not been as amused.

Admittedly, Roysa did not seem greatly amused by the story that currently had him in stitches. Idalia was telling them, in great detail, about her sister's first attempt to practice archery with her male counterparts. She had arrived at the training yard barefoot, as was the practice of many archers, and demanded a bow. Idalia admitted to not being present at the time, but her father had gladly shared the tale with them that night at supper. He'd explained that only those using a longbow needed to forsake footwear, the extra grip needed to steady an accurate shot.

Apparently it had not been her first attempt to train with the men. Her visit to the archery butts had been her way of rebutting her father's denial of her request for a sword.

It was the image of a young Roysa standing in her bare feet, likely in a lovely gown, among a group of full-grown knights that had made him start laughing, and he found he could not stop. Lance and Idalia both joined him, and Terric could not blame Gilbert for looking at them all as if they'd gone mad. Terric raised a cup to his marshal, who sat just below them, and though Gilbert raised his goblet in return, he could tell the poor man worried for his sanity.

"I would gladly show you how to use a longbow." He waved away the pudding and dried fruits, realizing belatedly that Roysa may have wanted them. "However . . ."

His three supper companions waited as Terric attempted to keep his expression neutral.

"I would require just one thing . . ."

He'd meant it as a jest, but the look on Roysa's face made him hard in an instant. The way she'd parted her lips told him she was thinking about being his partner somewhere other than on the training yard.

"What is it?" Idalia asked at last. "What is the one thing?"

Thankfully, neither she nor Lance seemed to have noticed the tension between them. Slowing his rapidly beating heart with a long, expelled breath that he did not bother hiding from Roysa, Terric turned toward his friends.

"I would only ask that she leave her boots behind."

His shoulders shook as Lance and Idalia began to laugh once again. Even Roysa smiled despite their teasing.

He liked that she did not take offense.

He liked much about her.

Her laugh. The way she spoke to Lance, as if he were her brother in truth and not by marriage. It had not taken her long to learn what Terric had known since that awful day at the tournament. A finer man would be difficult to find, and the sight of Lance and Idalia together, so happy, made Terric wonder, for a brief moment, if it were indeed possible . . .

"I'll do it."

Roysa broke into his reverie.

"What will you do?" he asked, having momentarily forgotten their conversation.

"I will leave my boots behind if you'll indeed train me with the longbow."

He thought of bringing Roysa to the training yard in Bradon Moor. It would be the middle of the summer, and she'd stand there barefoot, her hands holding a bow the size of her own body. Terric would stand behind her, instructing her, touching her with the freedom of . . . what? Her husband?

The thought was both disturbing and pleasing.

She waited for his response.

"You would be forced to remain until the spring. I do not recommend training barefoot in the snow."

Neither of them were laughing any longer.

Lance and Idalia had begun speaking behind him, talking of something else.

"You may be forced to do so anyway, if Dromsley Castle is under siege," he said.

"Will it be?"

At this moment, he wished it were so. He found he quite liked the thought of being in Roysa's company for months on end.

"Nay. A siege would be a win for John. We will proceed as if Langham and Ulster will both move against us when the weather breaks."

He did not intend to frighten her, but neither did he want to hide the truth.

"News from my scout, along with your information about Ulster's meeting with Langham, forces us to prepare for such an event."

"Will you gather more men? From my father maybe?"

"We have allies, including your father, but there may not be time to get them here. I doubt my men will arrive from Scotland in time either. And by crushing the northern lords first, especially one who founded the order that vowed to bring him to heel, the king might force others to reconsider their support."

"But you will try?"

Losing was impossible, for many reasons, but also because Roysa and Idalia were here. He would not allow any harm to come to them. He would not allow Lackland and his supporters to take this from him. They would not prevail again.

"I will do everything to protect Dromsley, protect the cause."

Protect you.

"You were right, Roysa," he said, lowering his voice. "I have been preparing for this fight my entire life. The king will not best me."

She did not hesitate. "I believe you."

Her unwavering faith was more than he had reason to expect—and it scared him more than any interaction they'd had before.

He'd not earned that faith yet.

But he meant to, starting this very night.

CHAPTER 18

Though Terric had not wanted to leave the dinner table, he'd noticed his retainers were getting restless. They would stay as long as he did, and so he officially ended the meal and excused himself.

He took a moment to speak to Gilbert, his marshal, and a few of the men, but his gaze continued to stray to Roysa, who sat with Idalia and Lance in the same corner of the hall where he and Roysa had sat on that snowy afternoon, drinking more than they should, learning neither of them fit the other's initial expectations.

He had thought her beautiful then, but tonight, in that lilac gown, laughing with him as if they had known each other for years . . .

Well, he found himself thinking of Guy, the friend who'd vowed never to marry. Guy had done things the wrong way around, of course—he'd married Sabine to save her from her unscrupulous guardian, and to keep her from divulging his secrets, and the two had fallen in love as an unintended consequence of their marriage.

He'd asked Guy, of course, how such a thing had

happened. His response had been to clap Terric on the back and say, "I fell in love."

A simple answer—too simple, indeed, given Terric himself had been in love before. Or had, at least, believed himself to be.

His sister had, in fact, warned him against the laird's daughter. Despite it, he opened himself to her. To Isobel's sweet words and stolen kisses. It was only when Cait very deliberately told her of the possibility of Rory someday becoming chief that he'd learned the truth. She loved the thought of being the chief's wife.

But not him.

He wanted to love his wife in the way Guy loved Sabine, and Lance loved Idalia. Something else had struck him tonight, looking at Lance and Idalia together. His friends' wives were a part of the order. While Sabine was an actual member, who bore the same mark they all did, Idalia was an honorary one. He *could* marry.

He was not ready yet, but neither was Roysa, just recently widowed.

However . . .

"Lady Roysa," he said, approaching his friends from behind. He did not wish to sit with them. What he had to say was for her ears alone.

When she spun in her seat, looking up at him, a prickle ran through his shoulders and arms. Terric focused on the single purple jewel that hung from her forehead, a favored headpiece he'd once thought pretentious but now adored. It gleamed up at him, as did Roysa, her eyes bright and welcoming.

"A word?"

She did not hesitate.

Gathering fistfuls of her gown, Roysa stood and smoothed out the soft purple fabric.

Terric avoided looking at Lance and Idalia,

knowing both of them were staring at him. They likely misunderstood his intentions. Of course, he'd not blame either of them. His intentions had not been honorable when she'd stumbled into his bed-chamber the previous night. Even now, as she took the arm he offered, Terric was tempted to guide her back there to finish what they had started.

What he had ended.

"There is an alcove . . ." He pointed through the hall with his free hand.

"I worried for a moment you meant to abscond with me back to your chamber."

"The idea worries you?"

Terric could not remember ever having felt such contentment as he did with Roysa on his arm. And on the precipice of a battle his own marshal and captain likely doubted he could win.

"Nay," she admitted. "It does not."

Grabbing a standing candle just before they stepped out of the hall, Terric guided her toward the most private place he could think of that was not his bedchamber. Or his solar. Both were too private, and Terric didn't trust himself.

Nodding to a watchman who passed them on the way to his station, Terric led Roysa toward their des-tination.

"This way."

Reluctantly, he released her arm and stepped in front of her. The stairwell was dimly lit, and she'd need his light to guide them.

"I've not been in this section of the castle before."

"Chapel Tower," he said, arriving on the first floor.

"A peculiar name as the chapel is not located here."

Terric could see their destination from the entry-way. A window seat in the largest alcove in the castle.

He suspected it had been built for the clergy who'd resided at Dromsley at the time.

"Oh my!"

Terric had been waiting for her reaction. A window such as this was so rare that Terric had never seen its like anywhere but Dromsley.

"This must have cost a fortune. I've never seen so much glass in one place before. I can see straight through it into the inner ward."

Placing the candle on the floor, Terric gestured for Roysa to sit on the velvet cushioned seat and settled down beside her. Through the X pattern in the glass, Roysa watched as the snow fell, once again, just outside. A nearly full moon provided enough light for them to see beyond the window, but not much farther.

"And it's warm," she said softly, looking at him in wonder.

Terric would have brought her here earlier had he realized she would have such a reaction.

"Do you see those gaps"—he pointed to the ground beneath them—"just there?"

"Aye," she said, lifting her eyes to see the barely visible gaps.

"Built there intentionally along this entire wall. We're just above the only fireplace bigger than the one in the lord's chamber."

"Bigger than . . . oh. The kitchen?"

Terric did not want to talk about castle design. He wished to ask her a question that had been burning in his mind half the evening.

Roysa shifted, adjusting her gown. Terric wanted to scoop her up and carry her back to his bedchamber, but instead he gathered himself and said, "I will see little of you these next few days."

She turned toward the courtyard, and just then, he could imagine having her painted. The look of wonder in her eyes, the way she was sitting so prettily on the bench, her gown impeccable. He faltered. Roysa could have any man she desired. And though she'd sent a message ahead to Stanton, she had not yet spoken to her parents about all that had happened.

Very likely, Lord Stanton would already have a suitor in mind. Of course, it would be Roysa's right as a widow to accept or reject his suggestion.

Roysa waited for him to continue.

"The upcoming battle, if it indeed comes to pass, will be hard-won."

"But not impossible?"

"Nay. Not impossible."

The last time Terric had been this nervous, he'd been facing down a rival clan, hoping he could avoid a pike in his gut.

He could not resist any longer. Terric reached out and took Roysa's hand. Pulling it onto his lap, he covered it with both of his.

"When we are able to steal a few moments, like this one . . ."

Terric decided at that moment that the scent of orange blossoms was his new favorite, replacing that of freshly cut leather. He breathed it in, pushed out thoughts of the following morning's war council, and forged ahead.

"Roysa," he started anew. "I have a question to ask."

CHAPTER 19

This was a side of Terric Kennaugh she had not seen before.

Granted, she'd only known the man a few days. And in that time she had despised him, gotten drunk with him, kissed him, and shared more of her life than she'd planned. All of those encounters had been quite different from one another, but they shared one common theme—Terric was a man who did not waver. All he did, he did with conviction, with the confidence of a man accustomed to leading.

But as he cradled her hand, looking her in the eye, he seemed less like the man who was a leader in two countries. At this moment, he was simply a man holding her hand. A man who appeared almost nervous, which Roysa had not thought possible.

"A question?" she repeated, attempting to imagine what that question could be. Would he ask her to leave ahead of the battle? After all, she had no real place here. Surely Dromsley was nearly as unsafe for her as Stokesay Castle, if battle was indeed imminent. Well, she'd not do it. Roysa refused to leave while Idalia was still here. So her answer would be a firm no.

"Will you give me permission to court you?"

Shock flooded her. Surely he had not asked . . .

"Last eve," she managed to get out, "you said—"

"I was wrong."

Had she really thought Terric like her father? Her father had never, to her knowledge, admitted to being wrong about anything. Nor could Roysa imagine him doing so.

Nay, Terric might be every bit as much a natural leader as her father, but he was a different man. Very different.

And he wants to court me.

"I . . ."

What could she say?

"I am recently widowed."

"But you are not in mourning."

Nay, she was not. Indeed, the brother-in-law of the man she'd married could very well be planning to attack Dromsley. None here would condemn her.

"Your mission."

"Will not be compromised. I'm asking merely that we learn more of each other, properly. I would not dishonor your sister and Lance by dallying with you, but neither am I willing to avoid your company either."

She was free to make her own decisions now, even if her father or others might not approve of them. Her father had often spoken of the decisions he was called upon to make as a baron. To decide, he'd told her, was to commit oneself to something fully . . . and hadn't she already done so?

Terric had stolen her every waking, and nonwaking, thought. Kissing him again, taking the pleasure he'd promised . . .

And yet, she had been wrong before. Not that she believed her sister's husband would befriend one so dishonorable as Walter.

But he asked to court her. Not marry her.

There was but one answer.

"Aye."

Terric tightened his grip on her hand.

"But you understand what that means . . . ," she said, her voice trailing off.

"I did not ask for permission to undress you. To slide my hand"—he moved so close to her they touched, the warmth of his flesh searing her despite the layers of cloth separating them—"between your legs and make you come apart with my fingers."

Terric released her hand, reaching up to cup her cheek instead.

"Or to watch your naked body writhe with need beneath me as I give you the very thing I so dearly desire. To be inside you. To love you so thoroughly neither of us is able to stand upright for a full day."

He moved his thumb to her lower lip.

"I could have asked for that."

Tugging on it lightly, he opened her mouth.

"I could have begged for you to join me this eve in my bedchamber, promising pleasures our bodies were designed to create."

He was relentless. And she wanted more.

"I could have asked for you to touch my thumb with your tongue." She did it the moment the words left his mouth, tasting the salt remaining there from their meal. "For you to wrap your luscious lips around it . . ."

Again, she complied.

"And suck."

Was she really doing such a thing? And did it really give him as much pleasure as it did her? Apparently so. Terric closed his eyes for a brief moment, and when he opened them, Roysa stopped.

Her heart hammered at his expression. Such longing . . . and for her. So different from the lust in the eyes of the men who had come to Stanton to court her. A warmth in Terric's made her glad for his question, and assured of her answer.

"But you did not," she managed as his hand moved from her cheek to behind her neck.

"Nay," he admitted. "I did not."

Terric looked into her eyes.

"I asked for permission to court you. And now that you have given it, I believe I will start now."

He pulled her close, kissing her just as he'd done the night before. But this time she knew how to meet his slanted lips, his insistent tongue. She kissed him back, her fingers weaving through his shoulder-length hair.

It did not last long enough. When he pulled away, she was fairly panting, her chest heaving up and down.

Roysa wanted more.

"We will do it the right way, out of respect for your sister and Lance."

The right way. Which meant . . .

"But you kissed me," she said, her voice much more petulant than she would have liked. To court her properly, there would be no more of that for now. But forging a marriage was the reason for courting, was it not?

And she had said yes. She had just agreed to potentially marry, sometime in the future, a man she hardly knew. Hadn't she made this mistake with Walter? She'd rushed into marriage with him, only to learn he was a very different man than she'd thought. And yet, she didn't regret her decision at all.

"A minor indiscretion. But I agree, kissing, as you just saw, is much too dangerous." He smiled. "If we are to do this as we ought to."

Roysa changed her mind. Her first instinct had been correct.

This man was quite unkind.

CHAPTER 20

"You asked her . . . can you repeat that?"

It was the first time Terric had smiled all day. There was little to be joyful about when planning a defense against a force that might be, by their reckoning, nearly twice as large as theirs. The other men had left the solar for the evening, dismissed by Terric, but he'd asked Lance to stay back.

"I asked for Roysa's permission to court her."

"Court? As in for consideration of marriage?"

The jest among the four men of the order was that Lance was as even-tempered as Conrad was mercurial. Lance very rarely raised his voice, and Terric took some pleasure in the fact that he'd inspired him to do so.

"Have you ever courted a woman with the intent for anything but?"

Lance poured himself the first ale of the day. The pitcher had been delivered to them earlier by the same maid who kept appearing, it seemed, everywhere Terric went.

"I've never courted a woman," Lance said, "and you know as much." Giving Terric his back, he meandered toward the enormous hearth.

This had always been Terric's favorite chamber at

Dromsley. It reminded him of the lord's chamber at Bradon Moor. Large but not obscenely so. Well appointed, though simple.

"Aye, thank you," Terric quipped. "I would gladly accept an ale."

Lance looked over his shoulder. "I was distracted," he said, by way of an explanation.

Terric stood and made his way to the bright red table built into the wall. He grabbed the pitcher, poured, and waited for his friend to speak.

"She is . . . ," Lance began.

Sitting back down, Terric watched Lance as he became accustomed to the idea.

"You told me once—not long ago, if I recall—that you'd not have peace until your mother and sister were avenged."

"Aye."

Lance came back from the hearth, sitting across from him. "You know, we always wondered at the fact that you were so much bigger and stronger at each of the tournaments."

"As we all were."

"True. But you were, *are*, different."

"I am the only one with Scots blood," he said with a grin. "And therefore, the only true man among us."

Lance made a face.

"You trained harder. Longer. That summer was the last one any of us saw that boy with arms and legs the size of his sword."

The reminder was a sharp one. He'd been too small to help Cait, too weak. If the other boys hadn't been there, the outcome would have been quite different.

"Thankfully," he said, his tone a bit hard. "But I don't understand what this has to do with Roysa."

"It's true, I was not looking for love when I met Idalia."

"I should think not. You could have devastated our mission by seducing Stanton's daughter."

Lance ignored him.

"I don't believe Guy was looking for love either."

Snorting, Terric declined to respond. Instead, he said, "I did not say I'm in love with Lady Roysa."

"Only that you wish to court her?"

"Aye."

"With the intent to possibly marry her?"

"Perhaps."

"But you do not love her."

He did not answer. Terric had loved once and was unsure if he could say the word aloud again. But he had been very wrong about Roysa, so wrong that the thought of never seeing her again prompted this decision.

"You've not spoken to her father."

Terric tapped his toe, waiting for Lance to finish his barrage of questions.

"You've had only one mistress in all the years I've known you," Lance said, leaning forward with his mug braced between his knees. "She is a fiery one, capable of helping you achieve great things. Of becoming the warrior you are today. Of making decisions bolder than most. But"—his eyes darkened —"she is trouble too. Even if you decide you no longer want or need her, she sometimes refuses to leave. Even after you think you've satisfied her. Because she's become accustomed to your presence, as you have to hers."

"Just state your meaning, Lance."

"Her name, as you know well, is revenge. A rotten witch who will gladly curse you if you let her."

Terric had heard this speech before.

Many, many times.

From all of them. Lance. Conrad. Even Guy.

They believed his hatred of King Henry ran so

deep that nothing would ever please him but John's complete demise. Conrad had pulled him aside at the last Tournament of the North, when they'd first formed the order. He'd feared Terric would not be content to tame the king, their ultimate goal.

He had assured Conrad that while it was true he'd dearly love to see the monarch's head on a pike, he did not wish to end up with his own stuck next to him. Aye, he would be content to see King John's power diluted. To see the barons take back some control. To see him answer for his family's evils.

"She has been a constant companion," he agreed. "But again, I thought we spoke of Roysa?"

The look Lance gave him indicated he thought Terric a child who had not yet grasped the ways of the world. The way he often looked at his brother.

"I can see you like her."

"There's much to like."

"Desire her."

He did not deny it. How could he?

"But would you really marry her, if the courtship was amicable?"

"I would not disrespect you, or Idalia, by dallying with her sister."

"You are an honorable man, Terric. The most honorable among us." He sat up straighter in his chair. "But is there room for love in your heart when your other mistress is so demanding of your attention?"

"After this battle—"

"There will be more. Even if he doesn't attack, even if he does as we've asked, he will never, ever let us rest. We are the men who brought him to heel. How do you suppose he will treat us, his disloyal subjects?"

Terric knew his friend was right. If they were successful, they would feel the bite of wrath as long as John was their king.

Lance downed the remainder of his ale, saying nothing.

"I can have both."

Lance shrugged. "Aye, a man can have a wife, and a mistress. But does it make for a happy marriage?"

"It seems we may find out."

CHAPTER 21

"Do you find it odd the meal is being presided by two strangers to Dromsley?" Roysa asked her sister.

They sat at the head table in the hall, alone, as they had the day before.

Idalia looked down at the empty trestle table closest to them. Normally Dromsley's marshal, captain, and chamberlain all sat there. But not today.

"A bit. But there are plenty of other odd things about our situation, I suppose."

Roysa tore off a piece of bread. "Would it not have been safer if you and Lance had gone to Tuleen?"

They'd not spoken of Terric since yesterday, when Roysa told her everything. Idalia had been both surprised and pleased. Or so it had seemed at the time. Since their discussion, her sister had not broached the topic again, and Roysa had followed her lead.

"Dromsley is better fortified than Tuleen, or even Stanton Castle. Lance, the order . . . they will be the first on John's list of traitors to attack, if he were so inclined."

"As he seems to be."

Idalia sighed. "Aye. We had hoped he intended to

keep the meeting. But I suppose a meeting is in itself a concession."

"Which the king does not readily give. Concessions, that is." Roysa ate the freshly baked bread even though she was no longer hungry.

"Nay."

Her sister was worried. And though Roysa felt the same way, it was time for her to be the older sister once again. Although Idalia had grown up quite a bit, she was still her younger sister.

"I believe in him. In them."

Idalia did not appear convinced. "We have no notion of exactly who might be moving against Dromsley. Ulster? Langham? What of the rest of the king's supporters?"

"John has few friends here in the north."

"Aye, but enough to take Dromsley Castle."

"You said it was better fortified than even Stanton, which it appears to be."

Idalia took a sip of wine. "Aye, but Terric is not preparing for a siege. He and the others are planning a battle."

"They are preparing for both. No?"

"I suppose so." But her tone was doubtful.

She could resist no longer. "Did Lance tell you much when he came to bed last eve?"

Roysa had not seen Terric since their discussion. He'd been locked in his solar with the others all day today and yesterday, and had not taken any of his meals in the great hall. She'd thought he might come to her. But she supposed that would go against the vow he'd made. To court rather than seduce her.

"I was sleeping when he came in. And apparently when he left as well. I've no memory of him in our bed last eve."

Roysa could not resist giving her a teasing grin. Idalia lowered her head.

"My sister, blushing? Could it be?"

"I am not." Idalia turned to her. "You are incorrigible."

And because it was true—she was feeling rather incorrigible—she said, "Tell me. Tell me what it is like."

Idalia looked about, as if she feared they'd be overheard by the few retainers who still remained in the hall, and hastened her over to the fireplace in the corner of the hall.

"Are you asking that I tell you"—Idalia lowered her voice as she adjusted her simple kirtle beneath her—"what *it* is like? Did you not . . . did you and Walter not . . ."

Roysa took pity on her.

"We did. But it was about as enjoyable as turning meat over an open fire all day."

Idalia rolled her eyes. "You are no spit boy, Roysa. Have you ever turned meat even one day in your life?"

"Nay. But I've seen it done."

"'Tis not the same at all."

"You deliberately refuse to answer my question."

Idalia crossed her arms. "'Tis wondrous. If he takes care to give you pleasure, there is no feeling like it. Are you satisfied?"

Nay, more like frustrated.

"Will it be like that for me?"

She paused as a servant walked behind them, the girl who always seemed so taken with Terric.

"For Terric and me?" she whispered, watching as the girl walked past them.

"Do you truly wish to marry Terric?"

"Courtship—"

"Often leads to marriage. You told me just a few days ago that you had no interest in remarrying, did you not?"

She hated the reminder. Marriage, as she had

known it, felt like a prison, but she also did not fancy becoming the man's mistress. Or walking away from him.

"I like him," she said lamely.

"You desire him," Idalia argued.

"There is more to recommend Terric Kennaugh than his looks." She thought of his broad shoulders and thick arms. "Or his finely honed body."

"I agree. There is much, much more. He truly is like a brother to Lance, and Lance has few true friends."

Despite her new vow to live her life as she saw fit —and not to care so much about others' impressions —Roysa was glad that her sister and brother-in-law liked Terric so much. He and Lance would actually become brothers in truth if the courtship did, in fact, lead to marriage. Had they realized the fact yet?

But she also understood her sister's concern. Not so very long ago, she'd thought she disliked Terric, and now she was contemplating doing the one thing she'd sworn never to do again.

Giving control of herself, including her body, to a man.

"That finely honed body is coming toward us," her sister said, lifting an arched eyebrow.

CHAPTER 22

"Good day, Idalia," Terric said as he approached them. "Roysa."

She caught her sister's eye before turning in her seat.

"A brief word?" Terric held out his hand.

"Of course." She took it, the warmth of his touch leaving her bereft much too quickly.

The last time he'd asked her that, Roysa had not quite been prepared for what he had to say. What was he about to tell her now?

"We should not venture as far as yesterday," Terric said, leading her through the hall. "But I convinced Lance a wee respite would not be out of order."

"Did he take much convincing?" she asked as Terric opened the second door they came to just off the great hall.

"Nay," he said, stepping inside and allowing her to enter. "He did not."

"'Tis the buttery," she exclaimed, spying a chamber filled with wooden casks and barrels. Then he closed the door, and everything went black around her.

"What—"

He cut her off with a kiss. Though Roysa couldn't

see him, she could certainly *feel* him. His hands were everywhere, his lips moving across hers effortlessly. She did not hesitate to wrap her arms around his shoulders, holding on with everything she had. Thankfully, she had dressed simply this eve, the fabric of her low-cut gown thin enough that she could feel him pressed against her.

It struck Roysa that she felt safer here, in this darkened room, with battle-ready knights bearing down on them, than she had in months. She felt *protected*. Of course, she'd always felt that way at Stanton, but she hadn't realized how important it was until she'd left. Until she'd found herself a veritable prisoner in Stokesay Castle.

When his lips moved to her neck, Roysa offered it freely.

"This is courting, then?" she breathed.

"Nay, 'tis more. I need more."

She could hardly see his face in front of her. But he was there, his nose pressed near hers, his warmth more inviting than the hearth.

"So much talk of death."

Another kiss.

"And destruction."

This one, on the corner of her mouth.

"I needed . . ."

Roysa kissed him first. She knew what he needed —for she needed the same thing. When his hands roamed down to her breasts, she welcomed the touch. Pressed into his hands, even when his mouth moved lower and lower. Terric's warm breath alerted her to his intent, and he proceeded to tug on her neckline, just above her breast.

He explored with his mouth, and Roysa arched upward, silently begging for more. For everything.

The knock was so jolting, she nearly fell backward in her haste to jump away from him.

When he opened the door, her eyes narrowed at the light's intrusion.

"Terric?" came the fervent question.

"Lance, by God—"

"We have visitors."

Terric opened the door a bit wider.

"How did you find me?"

She couldn't see Lance's face but could imagine his exasperated expression.

"A wee respite," he mimicked Terric's accent. "I knew exactly what you meant when you suggested it."

He didn't wait for Terric to comment.

"A small party is marching toward Dromsley," he blurted. "Their banners are clear even from a distance."

"Who is it?" Terric asked. "Surely the king wouldn't send such a small group."

Roysa didn't need to wait for Lance's answer—he'd met her gaze and held it, but not as a reprimand. It was a message.

"'Tis my father," she guessed.

Lance nodded.

"Aye, my lady. Lord Stanton is here."

⚜

STANTON HAD COME TO DROMSLEY AS A FATHER. He'd received his daughter's message about her husband's death, and the sordid details around it. As such, he'd not come with a retinue of men. The second message they'd sent to Stanton, warning of a possible attack, had likely not reached the castle yet.

They'd quickly moved to the solar, along with Lance and Terric's men, and Terric now sat across from the man who, though he did not yet know it, might be his future father-in-law.

"Who else have you asked for help?" Stanton asked. Direct. To the point.

"Just you. No others but Noreham can spare enough men, and he is too far south," Lance answered for him.

"We've informed Noreham as well," Gilbert added. "Though it's to be expected he'll have his own battles to fight. If John truly is mobilizing, there's a good chance he'll start by moving against Noreham considering his role in sending Bande de Valeur back to France."

"Or with Licheford." Terric moved the map they'd been poring over for the last several days toward Stanton. "It would be a strategic win, to take such a place." And Conrad well knew it.

"But risky." Stanton leaned forward, over the map. "The earls of Licheford have a long history of victory, against all manner of foes."

"Though they've never had cause to fight their own king," he replied.

Stanton looked up, his eyes hard. "Nor have any of us."

Terric and Lance exchanged a glance.

"Tell me of your plan."

When Gilbert took over, Terric, grateful, only partially listened. Instead, he thought of the question Lance had whispered to him on their way to this chamber.

"What will you tell him?"

He'd not yet had the opportunity to speak with Stanton, but he knew he could not very well court Lady Roysa under her father's nose without first seeking the man's permission. Was he truly ready to marry her . . .

He could feel her lips against his even now.

For the blood of Christ, her father stands just next to me.

But now that he'd had a small taste, Terric wanted more. He wanted it all.

"Is there no other way?"

Clearly Stanton did not approve of their plan.

"A siege?" Lord Stanton looked at him.

"We could hold out for months, mayhap even a year. But by then—"

"By then John will have won," Stanton said with a nod. "A siege here would be akin to a victory for him. Word will spread," Stanton said.

"Our allies will worry," he agreed. "If the right ones abandon our cause . . ."

"It will be lost." Stanton crossed his arms as if surprised no one had gone to the trouble of arguing with him.

Satisfied, Terric looked pointedly at Gilbert, who had been against his plan from the beginning.

"Unfortunately, it may still be our best hope."

Terric's smile fled. Stanton could not mean . . .

"By your account, it does not appear they are waiting on the weather," the earl began. "At least, we cannot assume as much."

"Aye," he agreed. "We have been moving forward with plans to move out within the next few days. As a precaution. Though our scouts have not reported anyone approaching, we will set up camp outside the castle walls in an area to our advantage."

"My daughters?"

"We considered having Lance escort them to you—"

"But if delaying the meeting was a ruse for more time, we must also consider the possibility John will also send men from the west." Which was exactly the conclusion Terric and Lance had reached after days of discussing the matter.

"Aye. Which means your daughters would be safest here."

"You do not have the numbers to defeat Ulster if he brings reinforcements."

Terric would not allow anyone, not even Roysa's father, to alter what he knew was the best plan they could possibly have devised under the circumstances.

"Unfortunately, there is no other . . ."

He froze.

A memory had slammed into him—something his friend Conrad had said to him the day everything had changed. The day his sister's trusting nature had been shattered. The day he'd vowed to avenge his sister by striking against King Henry's line.

"I failed my sister," he'd said to Conrad, the one who'd ultimately slain the bastard who'd tried to hurt Cait. "The king's man knocked me down as if I were a young girl."

"Failed?" Conrad had said. "The man is dead. Your sister safe. If you need help to succeed, then take it. Burn a bridge, if you must, but take the win."

"Burn a bridge?" one of the other boys had asked. Terric could not remember if it had been Lance or Guy.

"Aye. Burn a bridge. My grandfather once held off an attack by burning the bridge over which his enemies needed to travel. There are many ways of defeating your enemies. The direct approach isn't always best."

Burn a bridge.

He had his answer!

"We will burn a bridge," he announced, his tone brooking no argument.

Lance shot him a curious look—although Terric couldn't be sure if it was because he remembered the conversation too or because he thought Terric had gone mad. Everyone else simply stared at him.

"The Watershed Bridge," he clarified. "Without it,

Ulster and Langham will have to travel far north or south to make the crossing."

"Or risk losing men crossing it before the thaw," Lance said.

"Either way," he continued, "they will be delayed."

"Giving me time to return with men," Stanton added.

"And my own men time to arrive from Bradon Moor."

That seemed to surprise Stanton. He needn't ask why—this was an English sort of argument, and they were men from Scotland. But they were *his* men. "Your clansmen are coming?"

They should already be here.

But Terric chose to keep that thought to himself. "Aye," he said simply, not willing to discuss the situation.

"Very well." Stanton stood up straight.

Terric looked from Lance to Gilbert. Neither appeared to have an argument with the plan. Although they would likely object to his next point.

"And I'll be the one to burn it down."

CHAPTER 23

"But you've only just arrived!"

Idalia stood next to her near the hall's entrance just after sunrise as they said goodbye to their father.

The previous night, the men had surprised them by joining them for the evening meal. Unfortunately, there had been little opportunity for a private talk with either Terric or her father. Her father's title dictated he should sit next to their host. Lance, as always, sat on his other side with Idalia next to him. And because the steward had seated her next to Idalia, she'd been too far to converse with either her would-be suitor or her father.

"Be thankful," Idalia had whispered. "They speak of nothing but the upcoming battle."

She'd hoped Terric would ask to speak with her privately before the meal, but he'd contented himself with a parting glance that Roysa had struggled to interpret. Was it regret? Longing? Something else?

She'd slept very little, and just before morning mass, Idalia had pulled her away to tell her of the plan they'd devised the previous night. Although the council had agreed to keep it a secret, Lance had divulged some of the details to his wife. She didn't know what Terric's mission was—only that he'd be gone and back in less than a sennight if all went according to plan.

Thinking of Terric, of the plan he had not shared with her, she'd fidgeted through the priest's sermon. Eager to see Terric. To talk to either him or her father. But neither of them had appeared at the morning meal.

Indeed, Roysa had broken her fast alone.

Only afterward, when Idalia had rushed up to explain that Father wanted to speak to her, had she learned why.

"He knows," her sister had said. "Father's about to leave, but he wants to talk to you, and he knows about Terric."

She'd found herself face-to-face with Father before she even had time to recover, Idalia's words floating through her mind.

"Why do you leave so soon?"

Her father looked around, as if assessing who stood within hearing. They stood just outside the hall, which ensured there would be little privacy if they spoke openly.

"Over here," Idalia said, escorting them to a more private alcove not far from the stairwell that would take him downstairs and out into the day.

"A plan has been devised. We worked well into the night."

It was not an answer.

"We know, Father," Idalia said.

He gave Idalia a sharp look, the likes of which he'd never once used on Roysa. She hated that her father favored her so openly. Speaking to him about it mattered little. He would simply chastise her for worrying unduly about 'such minor concerns.'

Minor concerns. Such as her sister's feelings.

She loved her father, aye. But Roysa would never understand him.

"Lance told me."

Idalia's answer pleased him even less. Roysa wondered what he would say if he knew Idalia had been invited to attend the war council? Lance had actually requested her presence. The only reason Idalia had declined was because Roysa had received no such invitation, not that she'd expected otherwise. If there were not already rumors of her and Terric, that would certainly have helped them along.

"Then you know why I must leave for Stanton. Immediately." His gaze shifted to Roysa. "Your husband is dead. Langham adhered to the marriage contract, but you left anyway?"

"There were rumors. That he had his brother killed for . . ."

Saint Mary above, please do not force me to explain this to him.

"Rumors."

Her father sounded skeptical, but she would not back down. He had not been there, after all, and she felt certain she'd made the right decision. "Aye, rumors. And given what we now know, it appears those rumors were true. Langham is clearly not worried for his claim. But then, why would he be if his brother"—she refused to call him her husband any longer—"was secretly opposed to John, and Langham is the king's man?"

She could see Idalia's open mouth from the corner of her eye. She'd meant to speak forcefully. Her father wouldn't have listened otherwise. While most lords might expect their daughters to be acquiescent, their father was not most lords.

"And you would remarry so soon. Without my permission?"

"Nay, Father. Terric—"

"Lord Dromsley."

"Asked for permission to court me, not to marry me."

"Permission only I can give." *ha*

"I am a widow," she shot back. "One who fled, in fear for her life, and who will not be forced to marry again. Unless it is of my own choosing."

For a long time, he said nothing. Her father had always had two ways of being angry—loud and eruptive or deadly silent. Roysa hated the silence. Lesser men had nearly fallen to their feet in repentance under her father's scrutiny.

"'Tis unseemly," he said at last. "I would take you with me were it not so dangerous."

Roysa's chest rose and fell as she held back the many retorts vying to be spoken. Anything she said to him now would go unheard.

"Father, I do not believe it is unseemly at all," Idalia said.

This time it was Roysa's turn to regard her sister in shock.

Idalia had never, ever spoken back to their father.

Who was this woman standing beside her?

"You approve of the match?"

Had they all gone mad while she was at Stokesay? This was the first time Roysa could remember their father actively seeking out Idalia's opinion. Though it pleased her immeasurably, Roysa worried about how her sister might respond. After all, she did not seem altogether thrilled with the match.

"I approve of Roysa's right to make her own decision. As I did. She is a widow with more rights than I had when you allowed Lance and I to marry."

She could tell the moment Father softened.

Just slightly.

"I must go."

"Of course." She nodded, not daring to embrace

him in front of an audience. She hadn't noticed before, but both Lance and Terric had joined them,
though each stood far enough away so as not to in-
trude on their conversation.

"I will say to you what I told Lord Dromsley."

Roysa looked at Terric without intending to, wondering when he'd approached her father. And what,
exactly, he had said.

"If the other wills it . . ."

Had she just heard him correctly? Had her father
just given them permission? Maybe even his blessing?
Being curt was his way, but he never relented unless it
was his will to do so.

"Be safe," he said, walking past them. "I will be
back."

He had given them his permission.

And from the way Terric was looking at her, she
suspected she'd finally have an opportunity to speak
to him.

❧

"COME WITH ME."

When he passed by her, Roysa stopped breathing.
This was the Earl of Dromsley, the chief of a clan
she'd never met. A hard man, as she'd always suspected. By the time Roysa realized where he was
heading, it was too late to question the sanity of what
they were about to do.

His solar.

"Do you think it wise—"

Her words were cut off as Terric pulled her
into the room, continuing what her father's arrival had interrupted the day before. When he
kissed her, Roysa forgot everything. The growing
resentment at the way he left her out of the discussions Lance so readily shared with Idalia.

Doubt at how quickly they'd allowed this to progress.

Nothing mattered except the feel of his lips slanting across hers, Terric's hands everywhere at once. Roysa kissed back, not caring about anything beyond this moment.

"God, I could do that all day," he said, breaking away. "'Twas not my intent to accost you like that."

When he licked his lips, still gleaming from their kiss, all of the things she'd wanted to say to him these past few days fell away.

Am I really as weak as that?

Roysa pulled away. She couldn't think in his arms.

"We've not spoken since yesterday morn." Turning, she walked toward the table, knowing it had been the center of the council's discussions. Picking up the corner of a large map, she looked back at him. "I know only what Idalia tells me."

Terric joined her.

"What would you have me tell you?"

"Everything, since you ask."

Terric exhaled. "Everything?" He pointed to the map. "Neither my mother nor sister care to hear talk about battle. My mother, especially, forbids talk of it at meals."

Roysa did not wish to insult his family. "Father and I spoke often of such things," she said, lifting a silver coin from atop the map. "What is this?"

"A marker, for my mission."

There was something in his voice.

"The one Idalia had to tell me about?" And because she could no longer hold it inside, she asked, "And what did you tell my father?"

Terric's smile made him appear almost boyish.

"Which question would you like me to answer first?"

She thought of another.

"And why have you not come to me these past few days?"

"Any others?"

"Aye, but you may start with those, my lord."

"My lord. I thought we'd agreed my given name would suffice. Or do you address all those you've kissed so formally?"

"I've kissed few men," she admitted. "But I'd expect you cannot say the same? That you've kissed few women."

"Is that another question?"

"Nay."

She ignored the grunt Terric made, concentrating instead on the remaining questions.

"Well, my lord?"

"Shall we begin with the last? I've not come to see you because I've been here in this chamber. Planning, as you know, for the upcoming battle."

"At night . . ."

A little smirk crept across his face. "Aye, I've thought of visiting you at night. Of waking you, climbing into your bed and courting you with my body, as unseemly as that might appear to your sister."

She tried to imagine what courting her with his body might entail, but as always with Terric, it did not leave her with the ability to think straight.

"But it would have been highly improper."

"More so than stealing me away to the buttery? Or bringing me here unaccompanied?"

"Circumstances have changed."

Roysa's heart fell into her stomach. What did that mean, precisely? Was he speaking of the mission Lance had mentioned?

"Which leads to your second question."

He reached across the table and took the silver

coin from her hand, his fingers caressing hers before pulling away.

"I leave immediately for here." He placed the coin onto the map. "Watershed Bridge. If Ulster intends to march on Dromsley Castle, as we suspect, he and his allies will need to cross it. Without it, they will face a delay. Long enough for your father's men, perhaps even my own, to arrive. The snow has finally stopped. And though it does not yet melt . . . we cannot wait any longer."

"Without the bridge? Do you mean . . . ?"

"I will burn it."

"You?"

"Aye."

"Surely you have many men who could complete such a task. You are the earl. Your clan's chief. What does your marshal say of this plan?" she asked, beginning to panic. "What would your brother think of it?"

"Rory knows what Gilbert does not. Once I have made a decision, I will not be swayed."

"But why put yourself at such risk? If they are closer than we believe, if you're spotted by their scouts . . ."

Roysa couldn't continue. Surely he did not mean to do this himself. It was madness.

"I would trust no one, with the exception of Lance, with a task of this importance. But even he did not offer. Lance knows me too well. He knows that I would never have accepted."

"No, Terric, you cannot."

Panic welled within her, as if time had ceased to move forward. If he did this, he could be killed. She would lose him before she'd even had the chance to properly have him.

"As for your father?"

Terric moved around the table, sidling up to her with a decidedly wicked glint in his eye.

"I asked him the same question that I asked you."

Which was what she'd assumed.

"He agreed. Reluctantly."

He stood so close Roysa could lean forward and kiss him easily. She forced herself not to. There was still much she needed to know.

"So why are we here? Surely you must be leaving soon," she said, reluctant to accept the idea.

"Very soon. But I'm here—*we* are here—because, as I said, things have changed."

She swallowed. "Such as?"

"This mission, your father's permission. I would not walk into danger without tasting you, Roysa. Without ensuring you wait for my return as a hunter waits for the perfect shot. Eagerly. Anticipating each moment."

Oh dear.

Excitement unfurling inside her, she asked him a final question. "How, my lord, do you propose to accomplish such a thing?"

CHAPTER 24

He'd meant to court her.

To act honorably.

Her sister, the wife of a dear friend, was just downstairs in the hall. Her father, likely no farther than the outer castle walls.

But Terric simply could not stay away from her any longer. Something about Roysa tugged at him in a way he'd never experienced before. It was insistent, painfully so.

Terric tried to be gentle when he pulled her toward him. Attempted to move slowly, coaxing her mouth wide as his tongue plunged into her sweet depths. But he knew time worked against them—and so did his lack of patience. His desire for Roysa had become so consuming, Terric feared his judgment suffered for it.

He had stared at the strings of her kirtle so hard, he knew the direction of the ties. His fingers moved nimbly to undo them, not pausing once for contemplation. Once the ties were freed, he tore himself away so that he might lift the heavy gown free.

Terric paused, both fists grasping a handful of fabric, and caught her eye. He cursed inside at what he saw there. Desire, aye. But she worried too, and he could imagine the cause. Thankfully, the bastard who'd hurt her was already dead—otherwise, Terric would gladly have done the deed.

He opened his mouth to tell her, to explain. But he knew a better way.

In one swift motion, he lifted the gown and tossed it onto the ground.

Terric didn't know if he'd hoped for an undertunic or not. This certainly made things simpler, but they still did not have much time. Not enough for him to fully love her. Besides, he had no intention of getting killed and leaving her with a wee babe.

But that did not mean he could not pleasure her.

"My gown!"

Roysa turned toward the table and looked at the pile on the floor at her feet. The view of her backside proved too enticing to ignore. Stepping forward, he grasped both breasts, pressing against her.

Roysa's gasp, and the way she gripped the edge of the wooden table in front of her, was simply too much. He wanted to hear that sound again. Needed it like he did air. Pressing into her, Terric whipped the hair at her back to the side, kissing her neck with the fervor of a man deprived.

"Terric," she breathed, tilting her head to the side to give him greater access. "I can feel you against me." He pressed harder. "I . . ."

She didn't have the words yet. He would give them to her. Another day.

Reaching down, he lifted her chemise and very swiftly pushed aside the last remaining fabric that separated him from his goal.

"You will think of me," he demanded, slipping his fingers inside without warning. "When you wake." He began to move his fingers. "When you sleep."

Her firm grip on the table pleased him.

"I want you to close your eyes. There, now feel

the evidence of my need for you." He circled his hips. "Imagine me inside you, as I will be when I return."

From the way she moaned and clenched around him, he knew Roysa was desperate for release, though she'd never known it before. Had no idea how close she was to the blissful taste of heaven she was about to experience. Just thinking of it made Terric realize he had to finish this quickly.

Or risk coming inside his trewes. He was hard. Ready.

"Can you feel your own wetness on me?"

He used his thumb then, and knew she was close.

"This is for me, Roysa. For me alone. And when I return"—he licked and nipped at her ear, tormenting both of them—"you will know more of me than what I'm able to give today."

She screamed his name. Not *my lord* or *Chief* but his given name, so blessedly sweet on her lips. He stopped then, allowing her time to enjoy. To recover. To understand . . .

This was the pleasure she should have known as a wife.

This was the pleasure he would give her when he returned.

Groaning at the loss as he pulled away, Terric looked down. He could not go marching into the hall to announce his departure on a mission to save Dromsley . . .

"Your . . ." Roysa had turned. And was staring at his hardness with wide eyes.

"Cock, love. Aye, I know."

He couldn't look at her.

"If you'll give me a moment."

"Shall I . . ."

Damned if he didn't look up, groaning.

"Nay," he said, trying not to think of her hands on him. Or worse, her mouth. Closing his eyes, he saw a vision of her bent slightly over, hands gripping the table as she pressed her backside into him.

"Talk to me," he blurted.

"Of?"

"Anything. Anything but this."

Terric took a deep breath.

"Once, when I was a girl, my baby sister, Tilly, peed on my leg. I thought she had a covering on her bottom, but I was mistaken."

Terric's eyes flew open.

"Your sister peed on your leg? Whatever made you think of that?"

Roysa shrugged. "You seemed to be in pain. It was the first thing I thought of to distract you."

"Being peed on?"

"Nay, my sister. As a babe. That particular memory just came into my head. But I assume 'tis difficult to have"—she pointed to his cock—"that. When thinking of a babe."

It was the most outrageous of moments to realize it, but he could no longer deny it was true.

I love this woman.

CHAPTER 25

"Halt!"

Terric hadn't wanted to take any men with him, though his advisors would not hear of it. So he agreed to take one man to aid him. Though the bridge was only two days' ride from Dromsley, the delay would cost the approaching men more than a fortnight. Unless they decided to risk crossing it anyway.

Terric did not believe they would.

"Do you hear it?" A rumbling in the distance, barely discernable.

"No, my lord."

James was a capable warrior, but he'd not chosen him for his sword arm. No other man at Dromsley could ride like this young man could. His father had been a marshal at another castle, and James had practically grown up in the stables.

"We go on foot," he said, dismounting.

Terric's father had taught him to trust his instincts. And at this moment, they were telling him they should tie up the horses and get to the ridge. Grabbing the bag attached to his horse's saddle, Terric motioned for James to follow.

They were lightly armed, wearing the padded

gambesons typically favored by reivers for the ease of movement they allowed.

He'd not think of Roysa now, as the moment of danger had approached. He had done plenty of that these past two days. From elation over their last meeting to apprehension at the thought of Lance's parting words. His friend still did not believe he was ready to commit to a wife.

But Terric aimed to prove him wrong.

If his friends could marry in the midst of their mission, so could he.

Right now, his only commitment was to eliminate this bridge.

Terric reached the ridge just before James. Which meant he saw the problem first. The only cause for celebration was the dense brush hiding them both. For now.

Because their worst fears had just been confirmed by what he saw beyond the river.

"We must go back," James whispered.

His voice was tinged with panic, and Terric could hardly blame him. The sight of so many men, of Ulster's bright gold and blue banners alongside what he assumed were Stokesay's red and black ones . . .

He did not blame Lance for insisting they wait for morn. It would have been madness to travel in the dark on this terrain, with snow and ice still under their feet . . . but he should have left immediately. At dawn.

He should not have delayed with Roysa.

There was only one way for their plan to still work.

It had to work.

"James," he said, forcing the young man to look at him. "We will go down there, and _you_ will carry through with our plan. And when the bridge is burned, you will return to Dromsley and tell them. Do you understand your orders?"

James blinked.

"There is no time. They'll be upon us before I can burn it."

"Aye, lad. You can do it. I will delay them. Do you understand?"

"But, my lord? If you cross the bridge to delay them, and I burn it . . ."

He did not have time for this. "Do you understand your orders?" he said more firmly.

James opened his mouth, closed it, and nodded.

"Very good. Leave your horse here. Without it, they are still far enough away not to see you." Terric handed him the bag he'd retrieved from his horse's saddle. "When you return to Dromsley, tell them what has happened here. Now go." *uh*

Running to his mount, Terric ignored James's calls.

"Who do I tell? How will you return? Lord Dromsley?"

But Terric could not waste another moment. He rode as fast as the hill beneath him would allow, taunted by the sight of the bridge and the men beyond it.

The wooden planks creaked under their weight. *uh*

If he could not delay them, James would be lucky to escape with his life. Well, his scouts would warn Dromsley even if James could not. Terric tightened his grip, cursed himself for a fool for allowing this to happen, and rode directly toward the enemy.

too late

◈

"YOUR SISTER DOES NOT SEEM HERSELF THIS MORN." Lance clearly had meant the comment only for Idalia's ears, although Roysa could still hear him.

They sat in morning mass, Dromsley's chaplain urging them to pray for Terric's safety.

None were supposed to have learned of his mission. But the knowledge had spread, as information does, and his absence had been noted. Gilbert had finally told the men. Who had told their wives. Who had told the servants. In just two days, all of Dromsley knew, which was just as well, according to Gilbert.

By now, they'd have reached the bridge. If all had gone well, they would be returning home.

"Aye, 'tis very much Roysa," Idalia whispered back. "She does this when worried."

Roysa assumed *this* meant her gown. And headpiece. The extra care she'd taken with her appearance this morn. Unfortunately, it was the only thing under her control. Since she and Terric had not even announced their betrothal, Roysa had no purpose at Dromsley. She could not handle the castle's affairs or take inventory of their stores. Even at Stokesay her duties had kept her mind from her dismal circumstances and hope for a possible escape from it. There was nothing except endless days and nights of waiting.

And worrying.

"I can hear you," she whispered back. "Both."

Finally, when she thought she could bear the sitting and listening no longer, mass ended.

But something odd was happening. At first she thought it happenstance, that the chamberlain should look at her so, but others were staring at her too.

As they filed out of their seats, she said, "Idalia. They are looking at me."

Her sister put a finger to her lips. She only spoke once they were well beyond the chapel. "Lance, I will meet you in the hall."

He lifted Idalia's hand, kissed it, and bowed to

them both. It struck Roysa that he most certainly did not look like any blacksmith she had ever known. Lance's grey and deep blue surcoat draped down to his knees. And while it was not overly ornate, he did look very much like the lord that he was. With manners to match.

"Come," Idalia said, pulling her hand.

Although Roysa did not know where she wished to take her, she had another destination in mind.

"This way."

Taking a candle from the wall, she led Idalia to the lovely window seat in Chapel Tower. When Idalia spotted the window, Roysa bit back a smile.

"'Tis lovely, is it not?"

"Aye." Idalia sat, gesturing for Roysa to join her. "How did you . . . ahh. Terric brought you here."

"I cannot deny it." Nor did she want to. Those memories were sweet, and she wished she had more of them to keep her company while he was away.

"Roysa, what you said in the chapel . . ."

"I was simply being silly. I worry for Terric. For us." Except her sister's expression—was that pity?— indicated she had not been wrong after all. "Tell me."

"There are rumors." Her sister shrugged.

"Idalia?"

"I did not want to mention it, but neither do I wish for you to be unaware."

Roysa folded her hands on her lap.

"It seems someone has been whispering." Idalia hesitated. "That you and Terric . . . as Dromsley prepared for battle . . ."

Roysa put up her hand. She did not need Idalia to continue. They had been discreet—but not discreet enough. And she understood what people likely thought.

There could not have been a worse time for them to meet. For many reasons.

"I do not know how, or where, it began. Mayhap the day he sat you next to him? Or when we spoke a bit too loudly in the hall."

Roysa froze.

She knew how the rumor had started. Or rather, with whom—the young maid who so clearly admired Terric. Once, the maid's loose tongue might have angered her. But she only cared about Terric and all the people who were out there risking their lives for the order.

"It matters not. He will be back soon and—" Idalia took her hand. "I should not have been so hesitant with my approval. He is a man fully grown. As are you."

"I am a fully grown man?"

"Shush. Lance and I worry for you. He's known Terric much longer than I have."

"It will all be over soon," she said, wondering if hoping would make it so.

Idalia stood to leave, and she did the same. "Aye. Terric's plan is good. It will work."

Roysa held a single candle in front of her as they walked back toward the hall, moving further and further away from that lovely window and the memories it elicited.

"It will," Roysa agreed.

It will be over soon.

She'd said the words in an attempt to convince herself they were true, not because she actually believed them. But as they reached the entrance to the hall, she saw something that made her gasp.

Could it be?

"Terric?"

It was too soon. Much too soon. But he was there, speaking to Lance.

Roysa hiked up her gown and ran to him.

CHAPTER 26

Terric rode with his hands held high into the air. Even still, he knew the danger. All it would take was for one overly excited knight to unleash a rain of arrows on his head. The advance had slowed, at least. Which meant he was already achieving his goal.

They were far enough away from the bridge, the terrain uneven, that only the thickest of smoke could be seen at this distance. So long as James acted quickly, he doubted any of the opposing force would know what had happened until it was too late. His enemy now was time. Time, and the scout who'd undoubtedly been sent ahead. He did not see one but had no doubt they would have used one.

"Terric Kennaugh," he shouted, likely too far away to be heard. Despite his training, Terric's heart pounded in his chest as it did every time he went into battle. Taking a deep breath, he started again. "Terric Kennaugh, chief of Clan Kennaugh, Earl of Dromsley. I've come to treat with Lords Ulster and Langham."

One of the two men at the front of the group held up an arm. He estimated no less than two hundred men rode behind them, but all went silent at the gesture.

"You are a long way from Dromsley, my lord."

Terric could not see the man's face. All of the leaders were helmed. But judging from the way he held himself, Terric guessed he was an older man. Ulster, by his guess.

"Here to persuade you to turn back, Lord Ulster."

The man's hesitation meant Terric had been correct. "Here? An unlikely location for a negotiation, would you not agree?"

If the man guessed Terric was plotting something, he might send a man ahead. The scout would catch James, and they'd no doubt both be killed.

So much could go wrong, but he had no choice but to keep pushing forward.

"May I approach?"

There was a pause. Ulster leaned over to the man next to him—Langham?—and then straightened. The mere thought that this could be the man that had sent Roysa running to Dromsley for her life made him murderous.

"Without your sword."

Terric had expected the request but liked it not at all. Without his weapon, he was powerless.

Nay, not completely. I still have my wits.

Slowly drawing the sword at his side, Terric tossed it to the ground, thankful his father's sword was home, in the hands of his twin brother.

Riding closer, ever so slowly, Terric stopped just in front of the leaders. None of them removed their helms.

"You march on Dromsley," he said boldly.

"We march against your rebellion." That, from the man next to Ulster.

"Lord Langham?" he guessed. When the two men laughed, Terric reassessed the situation. If this was not Langham's banner, whose was it? He'd not seen it before, and from years of fighting at the Tournament of the North, Terric could name as many English coats of arms as he could Scottish plaids.

"Why are you here?"

He paused for as long as possible.

Hurry, James.

"I've no wish for a siege," he said, still watching Ulster's companion.

"You propose a battle, then?" the man asked.

"Nay," he said, with another pause. "I propose peace."

More laughter.

"Peace? By undermining King John's rule? But then, you are hardly an English earl, are you, *Chief?*" Ulster said.

Terric's grip tightened on his reins.

"I am a member of the Order of the Broken Blade. My country of origin bears no significance. Dromsley Castle is English. My earldom, English. Your king oversteps and will answer for it."

If he'd hoped to anger the men, and those behind him, Terric had done a fine job of it. They all spoke at once until Ulster demanded silence.

"I despise a traitor," Ulster shouted, clearly incensed.

"I despise a coward who hides under his armor."

Praise the saints. James, get it done.

Neither Ulster nor his companions took the bait.

"Your order will be crushed," Ulster scoffed. "Your rebellion with it. Go back and defend your *earldom* if you are so able. Our discussion is over. We will even allow you to leave."

Unfortunately, I cannot do that as of yet.

As much as Terric would have enjoyed gathering his sword and living this day, he knew he had not given James enough time.

"I demand for the others' identities to be announced."

"You demand?"

They laughed again.

The men's horses began to dance under them. The archers and crossbowmen all held their hands on their weapons. He could never outrun so many.

"You may demand whatever you please," Ulster said, "but you will receive little. Allow us to pass, or we will go through you, Scotsman."

They needed more time.

"Is that you, Langham?" he shouted. The man's hand moved to his sword.

Terric attempted to do the same, which was when he remembered he no longer had a sword. Nor did he have any allies to rush forward to help him.

He stood alone against a retinue of two hundred men, his only ally a boy who had, if he were lucky, burned down the damn bridge.

CHAPTER 27

Not Terric.

How was that possible?

Roysa could not stop staring at the newcomer who stood in the entryway to the hall. It was rude, of course. But . . .

"You are not Terric."

He looked at her, and for one brief moment, Roysa thought she was asleep. Dreaming. How was this possible?

There was only one way.

"You are his brother."

Terric had not told her he was a twin.

"Rory Kennaugh of Bradon Moor," Lance introduced him, much to the steward's consternation. Abruptly realizing his mistake, Lance stepped aside, moving toward Idalia.

"Rory," she murmured in wonder.

"Do not fret," came a female voice from behind him. "Rory is accustomed to ladies being disappointed he is not Terric."

A sharp pain gripped her in the chest. The woman who'd said the words was stunning, and although she hated herself for feeling jealous of a stranger, she couldn't deny she did.

Until she noticed the woman's long, dark eyebrows, her deep brown eyes.

Oh . . .

"Lady Cait, why are you here?" the marshal asked, clearly shocked as he took in the growing party of newcomers just outside the hall.

Cait. Terric's sister. She and Rory had arrived with his clansmen.

"Your clansmen have come to Dromsley." She said what everyone, save Idalia perhaps, already knew.

"My lord will not be pleased." Gilbert shook his head. "He will not be pleased at all."

She tended to agree. Terric would not be pleased by the fact that Cait had traveled here at such a time.

Everyone started to speak at once, creating a confusing melee, and Roysa took a step back so she could think. Terric had said his brother planned to send men once the weather broke. But that had only just happened, which meant they must have left sooner. Why? They couldn't have heard the latest rumors about the northern border lords loyal to John.

A familiar voice caused her to snap to attention. "Gone? My brother has gone, alone?"

Rory even sounded like his brother.

"We should speak privately," Lance said.

Roysa dearly wanted to be there when they did, but she had no real place here. It wasn't her right to insist on anything.

Rory agreed, reluctantly following the others toward the solar. She nudged Idalia away, seeing her expression of pity that she would not be joining them. "Go," she urged. "I will speak to you after."

As men continued to filter into the hall, the steward led them away.

"We've not been properly introduced."

Lady Cait.

Roysa hadn't noticed she'd hung back.

"Lady Roysa, daughter of the 3rd Earl of Stanton and sister to Lady Idalia." She nodded toward her sister's disappearing shape. "I believe you know her husband—Lord Tuleen, Lance Wayland of Marwood."

Lady Cait pulled down the hood of her mantle, and Roysa resisted staring. It was a difficult task. Terric's sister had a face so lovely one could stare at it for hours. Her hair was brown, with just a hint of auburn, and her wide eyes were honey brown. But there was something behind them . . .

"I believe the others are gathering in the solar chamber," she said.

Terric's sister did not move.

Silence held between them for a moment before Lady Cait said, "They talk of battles and sieges. I would refresh myself first."

Roysa understood. When she'd first arrived at Dromsley, she'd been desperate for sleep. Such a long, difficult journey was draining.

"Of course. Although . . ." She peered around her, looking for the steward. "I do not know this castle well enough to know where you will be installed."

When Lady Cait smiled, Roysa felt the power of it—it reminded her of Terric, the way his smile always gleamed in his eyes.

"Anywhere we might sit for a moment will do."

That, Roysa could manage. Taking off her mantle, revealing a vibrant green riding gown similar to one Roysa's mother had helped her sew, Lady Cait handed it to a maidservant.

She led Lady Cait to the very spot where she'd sat with her own sister earlier. The delight on her face assured Roysa that she had not seen it before. If Terric had spent little time here growing up, Cait had spent even less.

"Such a large window. And so much light." Lady Cait closed her eyes as if the velvet cushioned seat

148

were the queen's throne. "My backside thanks you," she said, opening her eyes at last.

"So will you tell me. About my brother?"

"Of course." Roysa watched as Lady Cait stripped off her leather gloves. "You know of the order?"

Cait rubbed her hands together. "Lance and Guy . . . and Conrad." She sighed. "I know it well."

Of course she did. They had met because of her.

"And of their mission?"

"I do."

They could see all the way to the stairwell, of course, and only bedchambers lay in the other direction. Roysa felt comfortable to speak freely.

"John agreed to treat with them, but not until spring. They've since heard rumors that the men who remain loyal to the king are moving against the men who signed the charter."

"Including Terric?" Lady Cait asked softly.

"Beginning with him, it would seem, as a symbol of the Northern rebellion on one of the order's members."

"And somehow my brother devised a way to delay the conflict and put himself in danger?"

Roysa thought it a remarkably accurate account of what had happened.

"Aye. He felt a siege would only bolster John's support. After learning the king's men here in the north move against Dromsley"—she lowered her voice, to be safe—"he rode out to burn down a bridge. One that would delay those marching against us."

"Alone?"

"With one man. He trusted no one with the mission, save Lance, who remains here at Terric's insistence."

Roysa thought the news might upset Lady Cait, but she took it with remarkable calm.

"When is he due back?"

Roysa knew the answer, to the hour. She'd thought of little else in the interim. "In two days' time."

"And your relationship with Terric?"

Roysa hadn't been expecting such a direct question from the soft-spoken woman.

"I . . ." She was unsure how to answer that. "I am unsure."

"But you do love him?"

She'd been looking out the window, but that comment drew her eyes to Lady Cait's.

Love.

Idalia loved Lance, surely. But they were the exception, were they not? She had asked her mother if she truly loved their father. If it was possible to love a man you'd been forced to marry. She had said it was, and she did. But she'd said it with a sadness in her eyes. There were different types of love, it seemed, and the love one might grow to feel for an arranged partner was not the same as love freely given.

Love was such a strange beast. A frightening one.

"I am not sure your brother is capable of it," she said.

"I asked for your feelings, not Terric's. But I can understand if you would prefer not to share them with me. After all, we've just met."

But she heard the message beyond the words. Lady Cait still wished for her answer—she waited for it.

Would she approve of her brother courting a lady so recently widowed? An Englishwoman, no less.

Roysa wanted to answer, but found she could not.

"Thank you for answering me, Lady Roysa."

"But I did not give you an answer."

"You did. And it pleases me well."

CHAPTER 28

Terric was dead.

He should have returned over a fortnight ago, but they'd heard nothing of or from him since James had returned to tell them he'd managed to burn the bridge—only Terric had been on the other side, facing an army. Each day was worse than the last. She knew she had little cause to grieve alongside his siblings. Or Lance, who had known him for over ten years. Or the people of Dromsley, who'd adored the son as much as they had the father.

She was no one, really.

But if she'd doubted her feelings before, she doubted them no longer.

When Langham had informed her of Walter's death, she'd felt nothing. Regret for a failed marriage. Sadness at the loss of a life, even if he had wronged her. But certainly not this all-encompassing sense of despair she felt from the moment she woke until her eyes finally closed for the night.

"Cait is asking for you," Idalia prodded, attempting to coax her out of bed.

How did she do it? Terric's sister amazed her each day. She knew how much Cait was struggling as well. To get dressed. To eat. To prepare for the upcoming battle. And yet she did it, without complaint. While Roysa could not even lift her head from the pillow.

She knew what it meant—she was the worst sort of person, whereas Cait was strong. Capable. She knew that, and yet it was simply too much to abide.

"I cannot."

"You must. She needs you, Roysa."

"Needs me?" Her voice rose higher with each word. "She no more needs me than you do any longer. I am nothing to her. To him."

Oh God, he was gone.

Roysa covered her face and willed her sister to leave. She simply wanted to go back to sleep. To forget.

"Aye, she needs you. How can you not see it?"

Roysa stared into the dark depths of her hands. Too much light streamed in from between her fingers, so she buried her face in the pillow.

"She's not seen him for nearly a year. You are her closest tie to him right now. It comforts her to speak about Terric with you . . . Roysa? Roysa?"

She had not cried after her wedding night, when Walter had so cruelly taken her maidenhead. Some of the pain could have been avoided, she knew from servants' gossip, if he had only given a damn. Roysa hadn't cried after any of his casual dismissals, or his painful, unpleasurable visits to her bedchamber.

Nor had she cried upon learning of his death. Or his infidelity.

She had not cried after hearing James's tale about the bridge, although the horror and grief had stricken her, changed her.

Suddenly, it felt like all those tears she hadn't spilled had welled up inside her, stored in her chest. They gushed out of her with the force of a raging river, and she sobbed in her sister's arms.

She'd tried so hard to make it right. For her sisters. For her parents. Her father. Even for Walter. But it did not matter. None of what she did mattered. Roysa was nothing but a widow who had fallen in love too soon and paid the price for her folly.

"He's dead."

Idalia said nothing. She may have rubbed her back, but Roysa couldn't be sure. She couldn't feel anything but pain.

Vaguely, she heard Idalia say, "We do not know . . ."

But they did, didn't they? Where else could he be? What else could have become of him?

Roysa didn't stop crying for a long, long time. She had never cried so hard, or for so long, in her life. When Idalia handed her a handkerchief, she took it. Tried to stop. To gain control over herself.

But she couldn't even control herself. She'd been naïve to think she could control anything—all she'd ever achieved was the appearance of it. Terric had seen that. And instead of helping him realize he suffered from the same affliction, Roysa had let him go.

She should have at least tried to stop him, although she knew him better than to believe it would have worked.

For what had to be the hundredth time, or the thousandth, she imagined him attempting to delay hundreds of men. Sitting atop his horse, a proud and valiant warrior, the chief of an entire clan with an earldom under his command. Alone. Knowing he faced death but doing it to save his people.

The sobs eventually faded, and her shoulders stopped shaking. Even so, Roysa could not force herself to get up. She was more tired now than she'd been when she woke.

"Roysa?" her sister said softly.

"Tell Cait"—her tongue felt as if it was two sizes bigger than it should be—"tell Cait I am sorry."

She might need the woman Roysa wanted to be, but certainly Terric's sister had no use for the one who could not even gather herself enough to leave her bed.

"I am sorry."

Idalia didn't move. Roysa wanted to tell her sister how grateful she was for it, but she didn't have the strength to lift her head. Instead, she kept her eyes shut, hoping, *wishing* for sleep to take her.

❧

"ROYSA."

She opened her eyes reluctantly, not recognizing the voice.

"Roysa?"

Groaning, she turned toward Terric's sister, mortified to be seen in such a state by a woman she hardly knew.

"I've a tray for you."

Breathing in the smell of freshly baked bread, Roysa realized she was actually hungry. But hunger wasn't the reason she sat up. If Cait could collect herself enough to come here, surely she could at least sit up in bed.

"I should be in *your* chamber with a tray of food."

Cait stood and fetched the tray from her bedside table. Settling it on her lap, Roysa eyed the bread and pottage hungrily.

"Please eat."

She did not have to be prompted, but even if she were not so hungry, Roysa would have listened anyway. Cait was small, but her resolve was not.

"'Tis night already," Roysa commented as she tore off a chunk of bread. "Idalia was here this morn."

"Yesterday morn." oh

154

"I slept through the whole day. And night?" Was it possible?

Her next question was answered before she could ask it. Cait shook her head. "There's been no word of Terric. But neither," she hurried to add, "has there been any tidings from Ulster or Langham. A scout returned this morn with no word of any movement."

Understandable considering the bridge had been destroyed.

"Did Terric tell you," Cait said softly, "about when he met the others?"

Her hand froze partway to her mouth. "He told me some," she admitted.

"It was a hot day. The hottest in many summers. And my first tournament. I was so excited to be there, with my brothers."

For a woman who had never returned to England after the event she was about to describe, Cait appeared remarkably calm.

"I should have never left the tents unchaperoned, but I did." Cait looked up, meeting Roysa's eyes. "Terric had never competed in the tournament before, and he was smaller than others his age."

Finished with the bread, Roysa attacked the pottage. Her mother would be appalled at her lack of manners, but she was so very hungry.

"I'll admit I wasn't confident he could win . . . I could not summon the will to watch. He was not yet old enough to joust or participate in the melee, but even one-on-one with the sword . . ."

She tried to imagine a small Terric and simply could not.

As if sensing her thoughts, Cait sighed. "Young Terric and the man you know are very different, but the boy and the man do have one thing in common. My brother never let anyone keep him down—no matter how many times he was knocked to the ground, he'd get up again. Even as his opponent laughed at him."

Roysa wanted to cry for the boy Terric. And for the man who was missing. But she didn't think she had any tears left. Her insides were simply . . . empty.

"He would never admit defeat," Cait continued.

Roysa understood her meaning, but surely this was different. Whether one wished to admit defeat or not, sometimes defeat was inevitable. Inescapable.

"James said there were over a hundred men. Terric was . . ." She couldn't say it. She cleared her throat and tried again. "Terric was alone."

"My brother is alive."

She said the words as if Cait knew something everyone else did not. Roysa could almost believe her. She *wanted* to believe her.

"You've endured much these past weeks. This past year. I think"—Cait leaned toward her—"having spoken to your sister . . . I believe you needed to allow your emotion to be released. When I returned home after the tournament that year, I carried on as if nothing had happened. Most of my friends and family back at Bradon Moor never knew about it. In fact, it was years before I confronted it. And maybe I never truly have."

Roysa finished her pottage.

"My mother was married before she wed my father. For love," she blurted out. Even as the words left her mouth, she was unsure why she was sharing them. Surely Cait did not care about her mother's past. "Her father forbade it, but she married the man anyway, and broke her betrothal to my father to do so. Her husband died, and my father agreed to honor their previous agreement."

Roysa pushed the tray from her lap.

"She cares for my father. But she does not love him the way she loved her first husband."

Cait looked at her with the same intensity with which she'd regarded her the first night they met.

"Does she wish they had never met? Your mother and her first husband?"

"I do not know," she said darkly, only then realizing why she'd spoken of the match. "But I wish it for her."

"Roysa, Terric is alive."

"If it's so—"

"It *is* so." Cait's eyes burned with belief, so bright and strong it couldn't help but be catching.

Roysa felt a weight lift off her. Although part of her still wished to stay in bed until they heard word of him, a larger part wished to take a bath. To dress. To wait for him to return.

If Cait, who knew him so well and had been through so much, could believe he'd survived, then so could she. Perhaps their mutual belief would have the strength to make it so—or so she imagined in that moment.

Anchoring herself to Cait's strength, Roysa tossed the coverlet from her legs.

"'Tis time for me to get out of this bed."

Cait's chin lifted. "Aye, Roysa. It is."

CHAPTER 29

"Roysa."

She dreamed of Terric calling to her from beneath the ramparts. Roysa stood with her sister and Cait, looking down and trying to find him, but she could not see him anywhere.

"Roysa."

His voice was getting louder, too loud for him to be below her. It tickled her ear, and surely that was his hand on her shoulder . . .

"Wake up."

It was no dream.

Roysa's eyes flew open, adjusting to the candlelight. Was she still asleep? Surely her eyes were deceiving her.

"Terric?"

She sat up as if she'd not been in a deep slumber just moments before.

"Terric!" Roysa threw her arms around him, squeezing to assure herself he was real. "You're alive."

She needed to understand how he had come to be here, how he had survived, but she wouldn't let go to allow him to explain. He held her as tightly as she held him.

Afraid this really might be a dream, though it

seemed very, very real, she asked, "Are you really here?"

ah "Aye," he murmured into her ear, "I am here. I am alive."

Her chest exploded and her hands began to shake. She clung to his tunic, tears coming quickly and freely. Cait had been right. Somehow, unbelievably, he had survived. And he was here. In her bed.

"Shhhh." His voice was the most pleasant sound Roysa had ever heard in her life.

She pushed him back then, needing to see his face. It appeared . . . unharmed, although her tears had rendered it quite blurry. She wiped her cheeks with the back of her hand. "You are alive."

His thumb assisted in the task, tenderly brushing against her lashes as Roysa closed her eyes and let him brush away the remainder of her tears. "Very much so, it seems."

Roysa didn't understand what he meant at first. When she did, her eyes flew to his. She'd thought of their interlude so many times. Every time her mind wandered back to that dark place Idalia and Cait had pulled her from, she thought instead of Terric's lips. His hands and fingers and what he'd done to her. She willed herself to believe it would happen again.

And now, he was here.

θ "Your sister and brother . . ."

"I just left them."

Roysa cupped his face. His strong, handsome, noble face.

"Terric . . ."

She wanted to tell him she loved him, that she'd been worried sick. But when he put his hands over hers, something stopped her. Roysa saw relief in his eyes, and maybe even love, but something else flickered in his gaze. Could it be regret?

"What happened?" she said instead. "And how have you already seen Rory and Cait?"

"Gilbert spotted me and woke them before I even entered the hall."

"And Lance?"

"Rory is telling him now. I will speak to him after I leave your chamber."

Pulling her hands from his face, Roysa pushed away the coverlet and sat so close to Terric she was nearly on his lap. She needed to touch him still. To assure herself he was very much real.

Grasping both of his hands, she said, "Tell me what happened."

He took a deep breath. "You know that James was successful."

"Aye," she reprimanded, "but only because you found yourself on the wrong side of the river."

"Indeed." He smiled, as if they weren't talking about the fact that he'd nearly died, and squeezed her hands. "There were around one hundred and fifty men. Led by two men, I believe. Ulster was one of them—"

"And Langham, the second?"

"I thought it was him at first, but no, not Langham. He never spoke or took off his helm, but I didn't recognize the banner. Red and black with three snakes in the center.

"Who was it?"

Terric shrugged. "I still do not know. Nor does Rory, but I'd not expect my brother to know as he's spent less time here than I have."

"Your *twin* brother," she pointed out.

"Aye."

That fact did not seem to please him. Roysa would ask him about that, and why he had chosen to withhold the information, at another time.

"How did you get away?"

She'd thought so many times of Terric facing down an entire retinue of men, alone. And could not imagine how he could have possibly managed to free himself.

"I don't know."

"You don't . . ." That was certainly not the answer she'd expected.

"As I told the others, I delayed them as long as possible. But eventually, they saw the smoke."

"And realized what you had done?"

"Not precisely. But it did bring an abrupt end to our conversation. Ulster suggested taking me captive. 'Twas what I would have done."

"To bargain with later."

"Aye. But the other man said something to him, and then I was set free."

Her eyes widened. "Did they say anything to you?"

Terric appeared as confused as she felt. "Ulster told me to prepare for a siege. He said we'd meet again soon."

"And he simply let you go?"

"Aye. I rode ahead of them, and only saw them once. A man alone travels much faster, and I suspect they spent a bit of time assessing whether the bridge could be saved. But I never did recover my sword."

"You were . . . you faced them without a weapon?"

"Not by choice."

It made little sense. "Why does he believe Dromsley will hold up under siege?"

"This castle was designed for it. I would expect the same."

"But you will go to battle instead."

Terric's eyes narrowed. "The king thinks to show our supporters how easily we can be overcome. I will not allow him the satisfaction."

"I still do not understand why they let you go." She paused. "Terric."

"Roysa."

They said each other's names at once, and something about his tone told her the joy she felt at Terric's homecoming was about to be tempered.

"What do you wish to say?" she asked softly.

"I missed you, craved you. Even now I can think of nothing save the feel of your lips on my own."

Roysa wanted to kiss him more than she wanted to breathe. But she held back, dread welling up inside her stomach. She knew he had more to say and sensed she would not like it.

"But it seems I am unable to control myself when I'm with you."

The answer was simple. "You needn't."

He groaned, his eyes softening. Roysa's core clenched in anticipation—the way he was looking at her said more than any words possibly could.

Terric desired her. Wanted to lean into her as much as she wanted him to do so.

But the look was there and then gone.

"I asked you for permission to court you. And I asked the same of your father."

She remembered clearly.

"Aye, you did," Roysa said.

"I would proceed with this, but slowly."

"Proceed with . . . this? What are you saying?"

"Ulster's men are one, perhaps two days, behind me. We must prepare."

"Terric? What are you saying?"

"The king must be defeated."

Roysa's heart began beating faster, and faster yet.

"Aye, of course, but . . ." She had no words. He was here, alive, but she felt him slipping away from her.

He released her hands.

"You should rest."

"*Rest?* Terric, I don't understand."

He stood. "I care for you, Roysa."

"I *love* you, Terric."

There, she'd said it. Just as she'd wanted to—needed to—from the moment he woke her.

"I love you," she repeated, "but I do not want to be courted by you. I wish to *be* with you. This night and every night."

She was no longer afraid of her feelings. The fear of losing him had opened her eyes. She loved him, and he was here. Alive. Did anything else truly matter?

"Terric . . ."

"I am sorry, Roysa. Truly. I am."

He left as quickly as he'd come. Roysa sat staring at her door as it closed. Tears welled in her eyes, but she refused to let them fall. She'd done enough of that already.

Terric was as afraid, maybe more so, than she had been.

Nay, not afraid. Distracted. Understandable, given the circumstances. But he did care for her, and there was no question he desired her. She would not become upset simply because she could not control this situation. She would stay calm and give Terric the time he needed.

CHAPTER 30

"Saint Rosalina in Heaven!" Roysa shouted from behind him, the words bringing him to a stop.

Terric deserved her ire.

He had avoided her all day as they made final preparations for battle in his solar. When there was no more to do—the scouts had marched out and the plans had been drawn up—Rory and Lance had insisted on taking dinner in the hall, saying they were as prepared as they could possibly be.

He'd hesitated.

Where Roysa was concerned, his training, his discipline . . . none of it seemed to matter. She occupied a larger place in his mind, his heart, then he could give her just now. Riding back to Dromsley, he had decided that he would do best to distance himself from her. For now. He could not afford to be distracted. He had somehow gotten through the meal, but it had not been easy. His eyes kept straying to Roysa, and Cait who seemed just as furious with him as his lady.

Although he'd been pleased to see his brother and sister, especially since they certainly needed the warriors from Clan Kennaugh, he wished his sister were home safe. She'd refused to come to England for over ten years only to come now, when they were at the brink of war?

She had refused to explain herself. Or to tell him why she was obviously so angry with him. Except now he knew, didn't he? Cait and Roysa had become friendly while he was away—a thought that made his heart feel fuller.

Roysa let out another little "Hmph," and Terric turned to face her, glad they were alone in the corridor.

"I'm reminded of a woman who could not be consoled, one who nearly got herself trampled by her own horse," Terric said.

She stamped her foot, clearly infuriated by the reference.

Oh, he loved her like this. She was a force of nature.

"You are an arse, Terric Kennaugh."

"I disagree, Lady Roysa."

"Did you not hear what I said to you last eve?"

Hear her? Terric had struggled to sleep because of it. To be loved by her . . .

Terric could think of nothing he wanted more. Save one thing.

"We will speak after the battle."

The scouts had not yet returned, but they would be back any time. He needed to think on that, and nothing else. He couldn't let himself lose his focus. Too many people depended on him, including Roysa. Her safety depended on him doing his job, and doing it well.

"Which battle?"

When Roysa put her hands on her hips, he wanted to slip his own hands between them, pin her against the wall, and redirect all her passion toward him.

"The one with Ulster? Or the next one after that?

You have declared against the king, Terric. The king. Of England. There will likely be many battles ahead."

"Precisely." He was glad she understood.

"Pre— oh. I cannot."

She turned so quickly she slammed into his brother.

Terric froze. He'd tried not to watch her, and Rory, at the evening meal. He'd tried not to glower as his brother made her laugh. But as Rory's arms wrapped around Roysa's shoulders to keep her from falling, he could not shake an ugly thought from his mind.

Of Isobel. And her disappointment that Terric was not his brother.

Roysa stepped back quickly, and Terric's shoulders slumped in relief. He chastised himself for acting a fool, but he could no sooner have stopped the thought than he could stop the upcoming battle.

"You've guests," Rory said.

"My father?" Roysa asked.

While it was true Stanton should have returned by now, he could tell from Rory's expression the visitor was someone else entirely.

Someone unexpected. Which could be very good or very bad.

"A Lord Berkshire, according to your steward. His men are still beyond the gates. He is eager to speak with you."

"Berkshire?" The name was not a familiar one.

Terric looked at Roysa, who seemed embarrassed to have been caught alone with him. He hoped she wasn't worried about the rumors. Terric could give a shite about what anyone said about them, and besides, his brother was unlikely to gossip.

"Do you know of him?" he asked her.

She frowned. "A border lord, I believe. But I know nothing other than the name."

"Pardon me," he said, walking past her and trying not to inhale. But temptation got the better of him, as it often did with her. He stopped just beyond her, the scent of citrus blossoms familiar and pleasing.

He knew it was foolish—it certainly wouldn't help him keep his distance until this was done—but he couldn't leave without touching her. He simply couldn't.

"I will be just a moment," he told Rory, who nodded and left them.

Alone.

Hauling her against him, Terric lost himself in Roysa's lips. She opened for him, and he did not hesitate. He used his mouth, his tongue, to tell her what he could not.

He loved this woman with a ferocity that made him reckless.

Pulling away, Terric continued toward the hall without looking back.

Saint Rosalina indeed.

৩৯৫

"Welcome to Dromsley Castle." Terric ushered the stranger into his solar, flanked by Lance, Rory, and Gilbert. The man had given up his sword without complaint, but they were all still a bit wary. With good reason. Their visitor had refused to explain his visit to any save Terric.

"I would have waited till morn," Berkshire said as he entered the room, "but fear there is no time."

The man's tone gave Terric pause. As did his late-night arrival.

"Sit," he said, nodding to the chambermaid, who had brought ale in behind them. She moved to Berkshire, extending her hands to take his mantle.

When he removed it, Terric stared at the man's chest in shock.

"Brother?" Rory's concern was evident.

But Terric did not respond. Instead, he shifted his gaze up to the newcomer's face. "You."

The man had not attempted to hide the coat of arms on his surcoat, which was the only reason Terric had not drawn his weapon. The man could have easily taken it off before coming here.

"Terric?" Lance sensed his unease and moved toward him.

"Explain. Now."

As he spoke, the others fell in around him. Rory, Lance, Gilbert. All knew instinctively Berkshire was some sort of threat.

"I mean no harm. Would not be here, alone, if I did."

Terric suspected that was the case, but he still needed answers. Catching Rory's eye, he explained, "He was at the bridge. With Ulster."

The others did not react quite as calmly as Terric had. Rory drew his sword, and he wasn't alone—Lance appeared ready to cut the man's throat.

"You'd best explain," Terric said in a slow, spiritless tone. If the man valued his life, he would do so. And quickly.

"I am but a minor baron. My land borders Lord Ulster's. I was imprisoned by the king at the time of your order's meeting for refusing to pay this latest wave of taxes."

"And you found yourself fighting alongside him despite it?" Lance asked.

Berkshire was about the age his father would have been had he lived. His eyes were thoughtful, and they never left Terric's.

"When I learned he was bringing men to Dromsley, I knew it was my opportunity to fight back."

Terric thought of the moment just after Ulster's men first spotted the smoke. When Berkshire had leaned down to speak with the other lord.

"You told him to set me free."

Berkshire's lips flattened. "Convinced him it would be cowardly to do otherwise. I assured him we were not afraid of one man."

"Why did you refuse to pay the king's taxes?" Rory obviously did not trust the newcomer, and Terric didn't blame him. The situation was unusual, to say the least.

The baron didn't flinch at Rory's harsh tone, another mark in his favor. "My only son was killed in Bouvines," he said, his eyes filling with grief and anger as he spoke of his son.

The chamber went silent. Only the sound of crackling wood could be heard, the mood shifting immediately from suspicion to acceptance. The Battle of Bouvines had been the turning point for the order. The crushing French victory in a battle none but John had wanted had been the catalyst for their rebellion.

"Did Ulster not suspect? Surely he knew of your loss and the imprisonment. Why would any man stand with his king, rather than against him, after that?"

Lord Berkshire raised his chin. "That I agreed to fight against you, and the others, was the only reason the king set me free."

That managed to surprise everyone present. "So it is true," Gilbert said. "King John commands these forces against us while he delays meeting with us."

"A meeting he does not intend to hold," Lance said angrily.

"Aye," Berkshire confirmed. "He could be sending men from the west and south as well. His reticence to share details with his barons makes me believe he attempts to do both—prepare for war and give the appearance of cooperation."

Terric had suspected as much. "Whatever happens at Dromsley . . . whether 'tis a decisive victory or a defeat, he will claim 'tis a local dispute. Insist he planned on meeting with the rebels all along."

"Aye," Berkshire said again. "You are correct." He smiled for the first time. "I'd not expected that delay. The bridge. Nor had Ulster. My men pulled away from Ulster in the night just two days ago. He will likely be here on the morrow."

Terric and Lance exchanged a glance.

"My men are ready to fight with you," Berkshire said. "Give me your orders."

Terric said nothing.

After some time, his brother finally prodded him.

"Terric? We must wake the others. What are your orders?"

Now that he had come to the moment of truth, he felt almost . . . unsure, something unusual for him. They had a better chance of winning the battle now more than ever, but was that the right move?

Or should they declare a siege, giving John exactly what he hoped for? Was his need for vengeance against King Henry, and now his son, swaying him toward the wrong decision?

"I need a moment to think."

"The men are ready," he heard Gilbert say as all four men filed out of the solar chamber. "For battle or for a siege. We are ready. You only need say the word."

A good man, that.

Then they were all gone, and silence fell. Terric was left alone with a decision that might very well break them.

He dropped his head into his hands.

CHAPTER 31

When the door creaked open, Terric expected his brother or Lance. Instead, Cait stood in the doorway, looking as she often did, somehow both vulnerable and fiercely determined.

"No wine here," he said, rising to pour her a mug of ale. "Apologies."

Cait took the mug from him. "Hosting guests has never been your strength."

Terric resumed his seat in front of the hearth. "I am as much a guest as you. This is your home too."

"I'd not have guessed as much from your reception."

Terric knew better than to answer. He had been a tad short with her, but he hated that she was here, in danger. He hated that Roysa and Idalia were in danger too. But thinking of them would not help him make a decision. One that was needed. Now.

"We can discuss that another time, perhaps."

Cait lifted her mug and then drank. "Perhaps," she repeated.

"You spoke with Rory."

By now, he assumed, the news had gotten around.

Battle. Siege. Whichever he chose, none would get any sleep this night.

"Aye."

Cait never did anything without cause. If she'd come here, especially given the circumstances, she had something to say.

"Go on, lass."

But his sister said nothing. Instead, she sat opposite him, scrutinizing him in her usual manner. Cait's silent perusal was infamous among them—it had even made their father nervous. But they all knew there was little choice but to bear it.

As stubborn as all of the Kennaughs, she would speak when ready, and not a moment before.

He braced for it even while considering his next course of action.

"Your advisors push for a siege," she commented at last.

"Some do, aye."

"Yet you prepare for battle."

"I do."

"Is that not risky?"

Over the past weeks, he'd explained his strategy many times to many people, but he would happily do so again if Cait were interested to hear it. She typically did not care for talk of strategy or war.

"Mayhap. Though I suspect it would be more dangerous for us to allow John to claim any sort of victory at this important juncture."

"How would a siege be a victory for the king?"

He took a large swig of ale and leaned forward, elbows on his knees. "While we sit here, doing nothing, he will point to the north as evidence of his power. Of how he has crippled two of the order's members and one of the most heavily fortified holdings in the north. Dromsley will be used as evidence of his continued strength. We cannot lose support now that our demands have been made."

Cait mimicked his posture. Never mind that she wore a gown. *? which was*

Mother would likely faint if she could see Cait at this moment. Nay, she'd likely already fainted upon learning his sister had effectively snuck out of the castle to join Rory.

"Or Dromsley Castle holds out, as we know it will, while the others continue fighting the rebellion's cause. The king claims this small victory but loses the greater battle, as nothing much matters other than his agreement to meet and sign that document you all prepared."

"So some believe."

It was unlike Cait to disagree with him for the sake of it. She'd always been more apt to do so with Rory. For that reason, Terric listened. "Go on."

oh "You are simply too stubborn to realize, in this instance, you are wrong. Although I suspect part of you does know—'tis why you sit in here, hesitating to give the order."

Cait never raised her voice, but it had the might of an army of thousands—something that imbued her every word with deeper meaning. It had always been that way.

"Your refusal to allow John this temporary victory jeopardizes your men."

"Cait," he warned.

"As well as Roysa."

He opened his mouth to argue, thought better of it, and closed it again. One did not win an argument with Cait. The only way to emerge victorious with her was to stop engaging.

"She loves you."

The only problem with that particular solution . .

.

"Continue to push her away, and you very well may prove successful."

Would ~~Was that~~ Cait would never relent.

"You've no obligation to me," she said so softly Terric almost missed it. "Nor mother."

"Cait," he warned again, "I've serious matters to consider."

"Aye, you do. And this is one of them."

Cait stood, placing her now-empty mug onto the table more gingerly than her mood would reflect.

"The king's father took our home once. And his man tried to take my innocence."

Pain at the back of his throat prevented him from answering. It was as if his tongue had suddenly swelled at her words.

"And because of it, you've become this." She waved her hand at him. "The strongest, most honorable man I know. A chief. An earl. A good son. And a brother that I've missed dearly these past months."

She walked toward him, extending her hand.

"But it is enough. *You* are enough."

He stood and took it. Tears welled in his eyes like unwanted guests he could only get rid of after entertaining them for longer than he wished. She wrapped her arms around his waist, but still he stood rigid—until he heard the sound of her crying.

Terric had not even cried when they'd buried his father, a man he'd loved above all others. But he did now.

"I couldn't protect you," he whispered.

"You were a boy. And you did protect me, Terric. It does not matter that you were not alone."

He hardly heard her words. Terric could remember the way the man, the soldier, had knocked him down with one push. His shoulder had been bruised and sore for days.

He'd been useless, worse than useless. But Conrad and the others had saved her.

"You owe me nothing more than what you've already done, brother. Can you hear me?"

I hear you.

She pulled away, wiping her face with both hands and sniffling.

"Why are you here, Cait? In England." He didn't ask it because he was angry anymore, or because he was worried for her safety, although he was. He asked because maybe now that she'd stripped him bare, his secretive sister would do the same.

"I will tell you, someday. As you said, you've grave matters to consider. But please think on what I've said."

The pleading in her eyes reached that dark, hidden part of his soul that he'd always refused to acknowledge. One which assured him that he was never enough—that he'd failed her and can never make up for it.

He could do that much for his sister. He could question himself—he could admit that he might be wrong.

"I will do so. Now"—he stood back—"tell the others I will be down to the hall soon. Either way, an announcement must be made."

"The hall was already filling when I left it."

"Good."

Cait's smile reminded him of their mother more and more.

She left without another word, and Terric refilled his mug and sat in the chair she'd just vacated. The advice she'd just given him swirled around in his head, along with that of his advisors. Terric was not too stubborn to acknowledge that his marshal, his captain, and the others who advised him had more experience than he did. Their input was useful. But every time he thought of John celebrating the decapitation of his northern rebellion, if only temporarily, rage boiled from his gut upward until it threatened to strangle him.

In the end, there was only one decision he could make.

CHAPTER 32

"It is odd to be in the hall and not at a meal," Idalia said to Roysa. They sat side by side in the hall, along with Lance and Rory. They were not at the dais but beside it. The dais itself had been cleared of all furnishings and awaited, as did the rest of them, for Terric to appear.

"There's Cait," her sister said.

Winding her way through the waiting crowd of men, English and Scottish, Cait finally sidled up to them. Other than a brief glance, she said nothing.

Roysa suspected she'd been to see Terric.

Terric, who'd kissed Roysa. Who'd rejected her. Who was alone in his solar, making a decision that would affect every single person in the hall. What a heavy responsibility he faced.

"Are you scared?" Idalia whispered.

She should be. But she trusted him to do what was right. "Nay. Are you?"

Idalia nodded.

Lance must have heard her because Roysa saw him grab her hand. She couldn't hear what he said to her, but Roysa was thankful he was there to comfort her.

"My father has gone to battle many times," she

said to Cait, who'd approached their table. "Every time, he returned. I have to believe they'll prevail."

"There will not be a battle."

Roysa startled.

"Dromsley Castle will declare a siege."

"They will?" The news surprised her. "But I thought Terric was opposed to a siege?"

Cait glanced at the others and then tugged on her sleeve. Roysa understood what that meant—she knew something but was not yet ready to share it with everyone—and so she followed her away from the table.

"To my brother, a siege is a victory for the king."

"Of sorts."

"Aye," Cait agreed. "To Terric, there can be nothing worse."

"Than to be bested by a king he hates."

"Aye." Cait looked toward the hall's entrance. "He's waited a lifetime to get revenge."

Roysa looked into Cait's honey-brown eyes. "He has good reason to want it."

Cait did not disagree. "But some things are more important than revenge."

"You're not worried the order's supporters will defect if there's a siege?"

"Lance does not believe they will. But I don't speak of the rebellion."

Roysa blinked as her friend's meaning dawned on her. Cait was a smart woman who knew her brother well. She had been right to believe he still lived. But in this, she was wrong. Terric did not believe he could have both his rebellion, his revenge, and Roysa—and so he'd walked away from her. Terric cared for her. Desired her.

It had not been enough. Although he'd claimed he still wanted to court her, slowly, she knew what that meant. If he wished to wait for peace, she'd become an old woman waiting. He'd kissed her, aye, and what a kiss it had been . . . but she suspected that kiss had changed nothing.

"He has already chosen," she whispered. "This time, you are wrong."

A cheer went up, bringing an end to their conversation. They watched as Terric made his way to the dais.

If he'd struggled with his decision this eve, none would know of it.

He really was magnificent.

A magnificent, bullheaded arse. But magnificent nonetheless.

Holding up a hand, Terric waited for the noise to quiet. When it did, he spoke, his voice booming from the back of the hall to its entrance.

"A force of over one hundred men makes its way to Dromsley Castle. With the aid of my clansmen"—he nodded toward them—"as well as Lord Berkshire, whose forty knights fight alongside us as allies in our cause against the king, we can defeat Ulster in battle."

A cry went up, of men prepared to fight. Of knights and warriors who had trained their whole lives for this very moment.

She glanced at Cait, who looked at her brother, straight-faced.

In battle.

Roysa's heart skipped a beat at the implications of his words. This would be the first of many battles to come. The first in a long, bitter fight against the king.

"But we will not be marching to battle today."

What had he just said?

"Though I'm grateful for your willing sacrifice, today is not the day you will give it. Dromsley is prepared for a longer siege than Ulster will be able to withstand. And while they languish outside our walls, our order's fight will continue against a king who cares more about the papal crusade in Wales and France than for his own people. And it will be victorious."

Cait smiled.

"Prepare for siege. Our enemy will be outside our walls too soon."

Prepare for siege.

Everyone moved at once. Some running, others shouting orders. But she stood still, watching as Terric stepped down from the dais and headed their way.

When their eyes locked, she asked the silent question.

The very corners of his mouth lifted, crinkling his eyes. He nodded.

To her.

And was swallowed up by Gilbert and Rory and Lance.

"I am wrong about many things," Cait said, reaching out to squeeze her hand, "but I know my brother."

CHAPTER 33

Terric sat for the first time in two days.
They'd needed to hasten to burn the area
outside the outer walls so Ulster's men could
not forage for supplies, but otherwise they were well
prepared for this siege.

Too prepared.

The presence of his clansmen and Berkshire
meant there were extra mouths to feed. Even so, they
could hold here well into the fall, if necessary.

And Terric did not intend to lose.

"The archers need to be resupplied."

Gilbert crossed his arms. "You're the only one
who has not yet rested."

Terric gestured to the bed upon which he sat. Not
his bed, to be sure, but he didn't dare leave the gatehouse. He needed to be on the front lines, near
his men.

"Am I not attempting to do so?"

Gilbert shouted a command over his shoulder.

"Attempting. You'll sleep as well in the gatehouse
as you would on the drawbridge, my lord. A proper
sleep. They'll not be building any more bridges this
night."

Courtesy of the wet moat, their attackers had

been faced with the choice of building a bridge or filling in sections to cross, given they did not appear to have brought a barge with them. Guards had been posted not just in every tower, along both the inner and outer walls, but also at positions between them. If any of Ulster's men attempted to fill in parts of the moat, they would know.

Bridges, it seemed, would be the key to winning or losing this conflict.

"No man can survive on will alone, my lord."

"Gilbert may be too kind to say so, but what he really means is you need to get your arse into the keep for a real sleep. Now," Lance said, approaching from behind the marshal.

"You will resupply the archers?"

"Aye, my lord," Gilbert said, "already being done."

"And will post new guards at all the stations?"

Gilbert and Lance exchanged a glance.

"Go. To. Sleep. Little will change until morn," Lance urged, his tone insistent.

Rory walked up to them then, his presence ensuring Terric would find no sleep here. He clapped Lance on the back, grinning. "You've the singular pleasure of being able to order my brother about. For that, I like you above all others," he said.

Terric stood, grumbling, and pushed his way past all three men.

"Remember the archers," he called from the stairwell, making his way out of the gatehouse and through the inner ward. More exhausted with each step, he stumbled into the keep. Circumnavigating the hall, which would be filled with sleeping servants, he spotted a maid.

"A bowl of hot water and cloth. In my chamber."

She curtsied. "Aye, my lord."

About to climb the stairwell, Terric stopped.

His thoughts turned to Roysa, but surely she

would be sleeping. He had so much to tell her, and he was hardly coherent at the moment. It would be better to visit her in the morning, surely.

"Cait?"

She'd just exited the chamber she'd claimed, just down the hall from his own.

"Terric. Look at you!"

Judging from her tone, he assumed she did not mean it as a compliment.

"Have you slept since the siege began?"

She walked toward him, but Terric stopped her. "I've a chambermaid attending. Go to sleep, as I plan to."

Cait cocked her head to the side, appearing ready to argue with him. Thankfully, the maid appeared, confirming that he had, indeed, secured assistance. "Good eve, little sister."

He didn't wait for Cait to respond and neither did she appear to move. Instead, she watched as he stumbled into the chamber, tossed his mantle atop the chest at the foot of his bed, and waited for the maid to leave. Except she didn't. She stood next to the bowl of clove-scented water.

"I can attend to myself."

Still, she did not move.

Terric realized he had seen the woman before, although he did not know her name.

"You are tired, my lord." She picked the cloth back up. "Allow me to assist you."

Terric closed his eyes, overwhelmed by a wave of exhaustion. The sight of the bed had made him feel every bit of sleep he had not gotten. He struggled with his tunic, but could not get it free—until he did.

Because the maid had helped him.

Though it was not unusual for a chambermaid to assist someone in such a manner, there was just one woman he wished to see him unclothed. And it was not the chambermaid.

"I can attend to myself," he said more forcefully.

Bowing her head, the maid reluctantly handed him the cloth. Somehow, he'd missed her look before. He escorted her to the door. "Good eve."

Terric opened it.

And no longer yearned for sleep.

Roysa stood there, in a thick, fur-lined velvet robe. Her hair fell in waves, everywhere.

She looked at the maid, who raised her chin in defiance and fled.

"Roysa."

She didn't need to inquire about the maid. Or ask if his decision about the siege meant what she thought it did. The look Terric gave her, the thickness in his voice as he said her name . . .

She stepped through the door, took the cloth from his hand, and waited for him to recover. When he did, he closed the heavy wooden door behind him, latched it, and stood next to the bowl. Next to her.

"Take off your shirt."

He did not hesitate. "With pleasure."

He continued to study her. But as soon as he removed his linen shirt, it was she who studied him. Every muscle, every indentation. Somehow she remembered to dip the cloth into the water.

"Come closer."

"Also with pleasure."

"I assume this is what the maid had planned to do?" When the cloth first dipped down to touch his chest, his muscles twitched as if in welcome. Roysa cursed the cloth for separating her fingers from his flesh.

"Apparently so. Though I'd not have allowed it."

Roysa continued to move the cloth along his chest and shoulders.

"Why?"

She had not waited for two days to act coy. Roysa wanted to know what Terric was thinking, and this might be her only opportunity to ask him. She wasn't about to waste it.

"Only one woman will touch me."

She dipped the cloth back into the water, took it out and squeezed. Somehow, her hands remained steady.

"Only one woman will know the intimacy of this chamber. Of my bedchamber in Bradon Moor."

Scotland.

"I will know one woman this night, and every remaining night of my life."

Her heart skipped a beat as Terric stopped her ministrations, covering her hand with his.

"There is only one woman I would court . . . until we have sufficient time to wed."

She moved her hand once again, wanting to feel every ridge of his chest.

"I'm not sure I want to be courted."

Terric's eyes narrowed.

"I do believe I would like to be bedded instead," she said boldly.

"Oh love, I will bed you. Mayhap just once this night, for if I don't get some sleep, my men are as likely to kill me as they are to follow me."

She blushed.

"But know this, Lady Roysa. Once will not be enough. Of that you can be sure."

CHAPTER 34

H is kissed her harder, longer than ever before.
Terric loved her with his lips, begging for
forgiveness he didn't deserve. Had he truly
been tired before? Before her arrival, thoughts of his
bed had overpowered all others. But now, a rush of
exuberance claimed him.

He wanted to touch her everywhere.

To see the woman who would be his wife.

Court her, indeed.

Terric would *claim* her. Make love to her.

But not with so many clothes between them. He
tore open her robe, tossing it to the ground so that
she was left wearing only a thin shift. "Oh God,
Roysa."

Never had he wanted to be rid of something more
than the remnants of fabric that separated them. But
as he reached for her, Roysa stopped him.

"Let me."

Something about the words, and the way she'd
said them, alerted him to a subtle change in her
manner.

"Wait."

Had he really said the vile word?

"Something about you is different."

He hadn't meant for it to sound accusatory, but he wished to know her better than anyone. He wished to understand her better than anyone.

"'Tis a long story."

"I've all night."

She laughed, the sweet sound a welcome respite from the whoosh of arrows whipping through the air, and from men's screams—it did not matter that they came from the other side of the battlements.

"Nay, you do not." She nodded to the bed. "Sleep, remember?"

"You will tell me when we do have time."

"Out there"—she indicated the door—"you may order your men about. But here, in your bedchamber—"

"Our bedchamber."

"In here, in our bedchamber . . . we are equals."

She defied him to deny it.

"Not equals," he said, much to her surprise.

Terric closed the distance between them. "You are lovelier"—he reached for the hem of her shift—"more clever." Lifting it over her head, he gave her robe a companion on the floor. "And in every way, you are my master."

If he'd intended to say anything else, he lost track of it. She was blessedly nude, and Terric could talk no longer. He divested himself of his clothing and kissed her. Swallowing her gasp of surprise as their bodies touched for the first time.

He needed sleep, aye. But he needed Roysa more.

They stumbled toward the bed, falling onto it, their bodies melding together as if they had been intimate many times before. Even though this was not her first time, Terric treated it as such. He gave equal attention to her breasts and the vee between her legs, his hands everywhere at once.

Though he positioned himself above her, Terric

had no intention of making love to her just yet. He sat up, his body protesting at the loss. But he needed to see her. He needed Roysa to understand.

"When I said you are the master here, I meant it. Anything you want, 'tis yours, lass."

He ran his hand from her calf to the inside of her thigh, his eyes on her thatch of curls.

"Tell me what you want, Roysa."

When his fingers found her, she opened for him. Her trust humbled him.

"I want what you did to me before."

He liked that she wasn't shy, and Terric gave her exactly what she requested. He leaned over her, propping himself on his elbow with his free hand as he plunged his fingers into her, tickled and teased.

"Like this?"

In a perfect position to lave her beautiful breasts, Terric used his tongue to caress an already-hardened nipple. When Roysa grasped the back of his head, he smiled against her. Pleased and very much awake.

"I've wanted this, craved this, for so long," he murmured.

Listening to her breathing, Terric knew she was close.

"Like this?" he asked, lifting his head to watch her as she climaxed.

"Aye."

"Tell me, Roysa."

"Faster."

Faster. Harder. He would give her anything she wanted.

"*You*. Terric, I want *you*."

Including that.

Pulling away his hand, he positioned himself over her. He paused for a moment, determined to erase every memory of the bastard she'd been married to.

Terric tried to move slowly, to give her time to

accommodate him, but Roysa was not allowing for it. As soon as he slid himself inside, his eyes closing at the sheer pleasure of having the one thing he'd been craving most, Roysa thrust her hips upward.

Terric's eyes flew open in surprise.

"I thought to move slowly, to give you time to adjust."

He began moving his hips when Roysa lifted one of her legs, giving him greater access.

Surely he would die this eve.

"In here, I am master."

He laughed, accepting the challenge.

"I said it but"—Terric circled, his buttocks clenching—"is it true, I wonder? Or are those roles reversed just now?"

Roysa's control was slipping—he could see it in her eyes. When her mouth opened, he claimed it, slipping his tongue inside. Her moans only encouraged him.

But when she grasped both of his buttocks with her hands and squeezed, Terric was lost. Having Roysa beneath him, being inside her. He could not hold on much longer.

Reaching down, he guaranteed he'd not have to, circling her nub with his fingers but not letting up anywhere else.

When she squeezed harder, Terric smiled against her lips in victory. One final thrust and Roysa came, tearing her mouth from his for the sole purpose of making a deep, guttural sound, which pushed him over the edge.

His body tensed and then released into her, Terric pushing one final time to ensure it.

He could not collapse without crushing her, so when he could no longer hold himself up, he rolled to the side. For just a moment he closed his eyes, reveling in the feeling of being with her, and then he opened them and turned to face her.

"I never knew," she said softly, reaching up to touch his cheek.

Terric had no words in response. He'd not mar the moment by mentioning the man who should have shown her, though Terric was glad he had not.

"Come here, Master Roysa."

Pulling her against him, along with the coverlet, which she lifted over them, Terric closed his eyes.

CHAPTER 35

"Roysa."

Fully dressed, Terric sat on the edge of the bed, whispering her name. He didn't want to wake her, but he knew it was unlikely he would see her for the remainder of the day. It might even be longer. He could not leave her without saying goodbye. Without kissing her.

"Roysa."

"Do you have permission to use my given name?"

Despite all that was happening around them, Terric smiled, remembering their second meeting.

"I do not remember asking," he said, repeating his own line.

Her eyes, barely open, began to flutter shut. Terric, reluctant to leave but knowing he must, touched her one last time. Laying his hand on her bare shoulder, he felt a wave of possessiveness.

"Mmmm." She turned onto her side, pressing against his hand as he rubbed the back of her shoulder. She seemed to enjoy it, so he was loath to stop.

"I'll gladly do this every morn," he said, Roysa acknowledging his words with a low moan of pleasure. She had completely flipped onto her stomach. Terric tried to ignore his increasing discomfort as he ran his hand from her neck downward.

"I woke you for a reason."

"Mmmmhmmm."

"Stay here. Do not worry about what anyone will think, or say."

No response.

"You are not a maid, and we will be married."

"Mmmmm."

"I will return as soon as I am able. Roysa? Do you hear me?"

"Mmmmhmmm."

She wriggled beneath his hands, clearly enjoying his touch. Would that Terric could stay. Sadly, he could not. Leaning over her, he kissed her shoulder, pulled the coverlet over her back, and stood.

He'd already added a log to the fire, so he gathered his belongings and turned to leave—only to find he could not. He stood by the door, watching her.

He had made the right decision, he realized. The only decision.

Terric just prayed they would stay alive long enough to enjoy each other.

Opening the door as quietly as possible, he slowly made his way from the chamber. Though the hour was still very early, the hall was as full as if it were midmorn. Guards who had been watching through the night had come in to eat before getting some rest.

Although his place had been set, Terric would not be using it. Instead, he strode to a serving maid whose tray was laden with bread and cheese.

"May I?"

Without waiting for a response, he took both.

"We've had provisions brought to the gatehouse," Idalia said, walking up to him. She'd been breaking her fast at the table.

"'Tis early for you to be awake, Idalia."

She walked with him from the hall.

"Lance woke me as he came in earlier," she said. "Typically it is my sister who arises first . . ."

She looked as if she wanted to say more.

He stopped just before the stairwell that led to the first floor.

"You've spoken to Cait," he guessed, remembering her remaining in the corridor. She must have seen Roysa as well.

Idalia's look of mock surprise confirmed it.

"My sister has never been subtle," he said.

Idalia was not very adept at keeping her emotions private.

"Do you wish to say something, my lady? Ask a question, perhaps?"

She shook her head vigorously. "No, there are more important matters that require your attention. Go." Idalia waved her hand for him to move on.

He did have important matters to attend to, but none as important as Roysa.

"She is in my bedchamber, as you already know. Still sleeping."

Idalia seemed nervous. He had not seen her this way before. "If you worry for Roysa, I assure you, my intentions are honorable. We will be married as soon as it can be arranged. Under the circumstances, of course, it might take a little longer than if we were not currently under siege."

To his surprise, that did not appear to be her concern.

"I believed as much. At least, Cait assured me of it."

Of course she had.

"What concerns you, then?"

"My father," she said, her expression tight with worry. "Lance tells me not to worry, but I cannot seem to stop doing so. He should have returned by now."

He could not deny it. The same thought had occurred to him.

"Lance said 'tis possible he was delayed."

"Or he may have learned of Ulster's arrival. 'Tis possible he is waiting to send word, to ask for guidance. He might not know we're under siege."

"Lance said as much."

"But still you worry."

She nodded.

"If I receive any word from him, you and Roysa will be notified immediately."

"Thank you."

A new wave of guards clamored up the stairwell.

"You are most welcome," he said, slapping each man on the shoulder as they passed him, their greetings—"my lord"—hanging in the air. When the last one left, he smiled at Idalia, trying to ease her worry and the shiver of apprehension he himself felt. "Good day, sister."

When she smiled back, her approval earned, Terric felt ready to face the hell that awaited him. Or so he thought.

CHAPTER 36

"How long do you believe the siege will last?"

Cait wrinkled her nose, making herself very much look like a rabbit. Roysa would have told her as much if they weren't standing so close to the guard. Terric had insisted they didn't need to serve as additional lookouts—that was the purpose of the guard who stood beside them—but both of them had wanted to do more than count sacks of beans.

Again.

"I would say until summer, at least," Cait said, shrugging.

"Longer," their companion said in a low voice.

They had been out here all afternoon, and until now, the guard had said not a single word to them. Not even when they'd attempted to feed him.

Since they were positioned along the inner wall, none of them wore armor, but Roysa had known him for a knight anyway. The way he stood, hand atop his sword as if the enemy were not well beyond their reach . . .

"Pardon?" Cait asked.

"Ulster has come well prepared and will likely receive reinforcements. It will be longer than that."

They'd spoken to Lance this morning, who had much the same opinion of matters. If John truly planned to make Dromsley an example of his might, Ulster would be just the first round of men to engulf them. Though his bridge-building attempts had thus far been unsuccessful, he didn't seem in any hurry to leave. No doubt, he'd send away for more supplies, adding to the trebuchets supposedly positioned outside the walls.

Roysa turned to Cait, raising her eyebrows. "You chose a fine time to return to England after so many years."

She'd hoped to catch her friend off guard, enough so that she'd offer her true motivation for coming, something she'd done against the wishes of her brother and her mother. Despite knowing she would also incur Terric's wrath.

"Your nose is red" was her only response.

"You'll not want to discuss noses. Yours did this." She attempted to recreate what Cait nose had done earlier, but not much could be said for her dramatics beyond that she managed to make Cait laugh. Even the guard seemed to smile. Maybe. It was difficult to tell.

Roysa looked out at . . . nothing. When they'd asked where additional eyes might be needed, she and Cait had been directed to the Middle Tower. But Roysa had begun to suspect this was the exact location where they were needed least. They could see nothing but the inner bailey and, beyond it, fields of white with occasional patches of mud and earth. She'd always assumed a siege meant the entire castle would be surrounded, but apparently that was not so.

"He hasn't said he loves me yet," she whispered, the one thought she'd woken up with. By now, all knew Roysa had slept in the lord's chamber the previous night. Though most of the women and children had been sent from the keep ahead of the siege, enough servants remained to have sufficiently spread the word before Roysa even broke her fast.

"He did wake me before he left. I could become accustomed to such a waking."

Cait's mouth dropped open.

"Nay!" she said. "He rubbed my back is all."

"Hmph. You've two sisters."

Roysa wasn't sure she understood how that related.

Cait gave her a rueful smile. "I have two brothers." She paused, then added, "But I am glad to finally have a sister as well. I begged my mother for one for many years."

She was glad for it too.

"Terric did say he loved you. In his own way."

Roysa thought of the man she had met, huge and brooding. And the man who'd woken her up so gently this morn.

"Do you realize . . ." Roysa stopped when she saw men running through the courtyard. "What's happening?"

They both looked to the guard, who appeared as confused as they felt. More shouts. And then she saw it.

A man being carried into the keep.

"Is that . . ."

Blood dripped onto the white snow beneath him.

Chaos erupted everywhere. "Inside. Get inside," the guard shouted.

She barely heard the words. Another wounded man was being carried inside.

Before she could properly object, the guard was ushering her and Cait through the entrance of the Middle Tower.

Terrified, they begged him for answers.

He said nothing before leaving, shouting for them to remain in the tower.

Roysa's heart thudded in her chest as he shut the door. She didn't know what was happening, but no one needed to tell her it was dangerous.

And she didn't know where her sister was.

Roysa didn't think. She fled back outside, hurtling down the wall-walk and toward the keep. This was the quickest path to it. Ignoring the shouts that rose up around her, Roysa continued to run until she passed the North Gatehouse. She ignored every plea to stop, to get inside.

She needed to see Idalia with her own eyes, to know she was safe.

Finally arriving at the Northeast Tower, she did go inside and nearly tripped down the narrow stairwell. Emerging from the tower entrance into the kitchens, Roysa ignored the servants' stares and begged to be shown to the hall.

"Idalia," she cried as if that would help her get to her faster.

Someone pointed her toward a door, and she thanked the girl before realizing it was the maid who liked Terric, the one who'd likely spread rumors about her.

It didn't matter, really.

"Bless you," she said, running toward the door.

"Roysa," Cait called from behind her. She hadn't even realized her friend had followed her—nor could she make herself slow down.

She nearly fell in her haste to get to and through the door, then down the corridor beyond it.

Once inside, she was met with more shouts, the screech of tables being moved, and more people than should be inside during a siege. Knights. Men-at-arms. Servants.

But no Idalia.

Calling her name, Roysa pushed past half a dozen people—and then her knees buckled and she collapsed.

"Idalia!" She also appeared to be frantically searching the hall.

Her younger sister ran to her and pulled her to her feet.

"Thank Saint Rosalina," Idalia cried, throwing her arms around Roysa's shoulders. "I was so worried. I knew you and Cait . . . where's Cait?"

She pulled away.

"Here," Cait answered.

Though it took her a moment, Roysa finally realized what was happening around her. The hall was being transformed, injured men being brought inside. But injured from what? Ulster's men could not possibly have breached the walls so soon . . .

"Idalia? What do you know?"

Her sister shook her head, but one of the injured men turned toward them. An arrow stuck up from his stomach. He was bleeding. Badly. Roysa tried not to look at the arrow, but it insisted on being seen, noticed.

She kneeled down beside him, holding out her hand instinctively around the arrow. She had no cloth, and he seemed to have been abandoned.

"Lord Stanton," he said. "From the rear."

Roysa's heart felt as if it had stopped beating.

Her father had come. Had attacked from the rear. And she did not have to be told what happened next.

The siege was over.

The battle had begun.

CHAPTER 37

"Finish it," Terric said to his brother's squire, cursing himself for not having replaced his own squire sooner. The lad's hands shook as he helped with Terric's armor.

"The men are in position, my lord." Gilbert stood beside him. Lance, Rory, all were armored but him. Impatient to move, he resisted shouting, knowing it would not help the squire finish his task. The aventail finally secured, he helped himself and grabbed his sword.

"Your first battle," he said to the lad in parting. It wasn't a question. He knew the boy from home, from Bradon Moor, and even if he had not, he would have suspected his lack of experience. The lad's eyes told the tale.

A healthy dose of fear was useful—men were killed less often because they were weak and more often because they were strong. As he mounted, Terric reminded himself of that fact. Even as he grew from the weak boy who'd been defeated by one terrible blow into the powerful man he'd become, Terric had never forgotten that lesson.

Size meant nothing without training. The ability to remain calm under pressure, and channel fear into caution, offered a soldier his greatest advantages. As the bridge lowered, his archers at the ready, Terric put all other thoughts from his mind.

His family. His clan. Dromsley. Ulster.

Roysa.

He discouraged them, one by one, and instead focused on one singular thought.

Remaining alive.

He could not train the men now. Instead, he would have faith in their abilities, in those who fought by his side. And, most importantly, in the arrows his archers used to provide cover for them as they streamed across the narrow bridge separating them from their enemies.

Screams washed over him. Screams from his men and their horses, and from the enemy too. Orders were being shouted, but not by him. Terric had rallied the men, given them orders. Now, they fought.

He would not allow Roysa's father to die.

Fighting like a demon, he slashed his way through his opponents. When Lance called his name, Terric turned in time to slice down yet another man who charged toward him on foot. He didn't know how deeply Stanton had penetrated Ulster's lines, but it seemed just now the answer was, not far enough.

Wave after wave of soldiers came at him. He'd searched earlier but saw neither Ulster nor Stanton.

"Gilbert," he shouted, watching as the marshal fell from his horse. He charged toward the man who'd injured him, intent on ensuring Gilbert was the last person the bastard ever injured. Once he cut the man down, he turned to look for Gilbert. The blasted helm made it impossible to see anything, so he tore it off.

He saw him then, lying on the ground. Dismounting, he ran to Gilbert's unmoving form.

"He's dead."

It was Rory's voice.

He's dead.

Terric had no time to mourn.

He swiftly sent three more men to meet their makers.

But it was too late.

୧୬ଅ

WITHOUT REALIZING IT, ROYSA HAD MOVED JUST inside the hall's entrance. This way, she could see each new body that was carried inside.

Not Terric.

Not Father.

Not Lance.

Not Rory.

The sight of all the blood, the gruesome injuries, had made her stomach turn at first, but not anymore. She paid no heed to the passing of time, moving steadily, following the orders of those who knew how to tend wounds, which she, admittedly, did not. Cait and Idalia were doing the same, each helping as they could.

Roysa become quite adept at staunching the bleeding from open wounds.

"No!"

She spun so quickly at Cait's scream—not Terric, not Rory—that she had to close her eyes to stave off a fit of dizziness. She opened them, her heart hammering as she peered a little more closely at the bloody body Cait was looking at. How had she missed him coming into the hall? Was it . . .

"Gilbert."

"The dead remain outside," the seneschal yelled as a reminder.

"Nay," Cait countered. "'Tis Gilbert. He will stay here."

Roysa could only stare. Just this morning, the marshal had chastised her for insisting on going outside the keep. He could not possibly be dead.

But he was.

"No. No, no, no."

If Cait's earlier cry had given her pause, this one was like being doused by a stream of icy water. She knew immediately who'd been carried inside. The wide berth he was given confirmed it.

"No!" she shouted, echoing Cait's words. She staggered toward him as he was carried to a nearby trestle table, although his sister got to him first.

"Terric, do you hear me?" Cait shouted.

"I hear you," he groaned.

He was alive! Terric was alive! She put on a burst of speed, reaching the table.

"You must stop doing this." Cait reached for one hand, Roysa another. He had no visible injuries, although she knew that did not mean all was well.

He answered with a groan.

She wanted to ask what had happened. If he had seen her father. If they were winning or if Ulster's men were even now within the outer walls.

But she didn't. He was obviously in pain, and she just wanted it to stop. Fortunately, Dromsley's physician arrived just then. He not so politely pushed both women to the side. While she watched, the man prodded Terric, who seemed to be waking.

"Gilbert? Is he truly dead?"

Before any of them could answer, Lance edged his way in front of them. "Gone," he said. "Go slowly, Terric. You took a hard blow to the head."

When Terric opened his eyes, Roysa could finally breathe. Pushing past the physician, she took the hand of the man she loved, defying the doctor to move her again.

Her eyes met Terric's—and she saw not relief in their depths, but regret.

"I tried to find your father."

Was he . . .

"Is Father dead?" she asked, that last word difficult to say aloud.

"I never saw him."

Terric's gaze moved to Lance.

"'Tis done," the blacksmith said. "Rory waits with Ulster to negotiate."

"Done? What does that mean?"

Lance might have answered, but her sister found them then. She launched herself into her husband's arms, their greeting hardly appropriate but very much understandable.

Finally, Terric cleared his throat. She'd do anything to kiss him now, as Idalia and Lance had just done, but his head . . . "Does it hurt?"

"To answer your earlier question, Ulster has surrendered. And aye, it hurts like the devil."

When he tried to sit up, the physician pushed him back down. "Lord or no, you'll be staying that way until the stomach settles."

Terric frowned but did not argue.

His stomach? Looking closer, Roysa realized he was quite pale. And did not appear well.

"Did we take any prisoners?"

"Aye, though they've not been counted," Lance answered. "The wounded are still being brought inside, the dead . . ." He stopped.

"Father is alive," she said, saying it with as much conviction as Cait had possessed when she declared Terric was alive after the incident with the bridge. Surely she would sense it if it were otherwise. And Idalia needed to hear as much. Her sister looked decidedly ill.

"Rory—" Terric began.

"Has taken command. You've nothing to fear." Lance turned to leave. "He will be glad to hear you're alive."

Terric groaned. "Felled once again." *ah*

He said it so quietly, Roysa didn't think anyone else heard him. The physician had moved on. Lance was gone. Only she and Cait remained by his side.

"Terric," Cait began.

"'Tis well enough," he said, sitting against the physician's orders. "The others took up my cause, and we were victorious."

She watched him carefully, but there was no anger. Or bitterness. Only sincerity, and she wasn't the only one to understand the significance of it. Cait's eyes filled with tears, but she quickly wiped them away.

Terric closed his eyes, took a deep breath, and then swung his legs over the side of the table.

"I must go," he said, reopening his eyes. His gaze suggested they should not attempt to stop them, and indeed, they did not.

Before he walked away, he leaned toward Roysa, pulling her to him for a kiss that was soft and filled with promise. The kiss of a man who had just lived through a battle that others, including Gilbert, had not survived.

"I'll find your father," he said, nodding to Idalia as he left.

And with that, he was gone.

CHAPTER 38

"Your men will be surrendered after the king meets with his barons."

This time, Ulster wore no helm. Unhorsed, standing just inside the gatehouse, the thin man with a slender nose to match responded with a sneer. "He will never do it." *ha*

Terric was inclined to agree.

"Then your men will rot inside Dromsley's dungeons."

In truth, Dromsley's dungeons had not been used, in Terric's memory. He had no intention of changing that now. The men would not be chained up, but they would be kept as prisoners. Best for Ulster to assume the worst, however—it would work to their advantage.

"By nightfall, any men who remain in the vicinity of my land will join the others."

Terric did not clarify if he meant the prisoners or Ulster's men who had died in battle.

"You are a traitor to your sovereign."

He felt Rory stiffen beside him.

"William is my king," his brother said.

Ulster snickered. "You fight for a cause not even your own."

206

"And you fight for a man who has no cause save his own," Terric replied.

Ulster was no longer looking at him. Instead, he had shifted his attention to Berkshire, who stood next to Rory. Terric hadn't seen him during battle and had been gratified to learn he still lived. His men, though few in number, had fought well.

"Traitor."

Berkshire said nothing, and Terric admired him even more for doing what he could not, refusing to let Ulster goad him.

"Where is Langham?" Terric asked.

The question surprised Ulster. "Langham? That coward will answer to the king."

It was all he said, but it was enough for Terric.

"Nightfall," he said, turning from the man who, in attacking Dromsley, was ultimately responsible for the death of his marshal.

Terric feared Ulster's attack on Dromsley might have also been the end of Lord Stanton—news he was loath to share with Roysa and her sister if it proved true. Something truly remarkable happened then . . . .

Stanton strode toward them with an easy confidence that made him question if a battle had truly taken place. Although his mail was covered in blood, Roysa's father appeared as calm as if he were sitting in his hall, awaiting a meal.

"Bastard," Stanton spat at Ulster, who did not respond. "Kind of you to remain alive." Stanton stopped in front of them. "Berkshire. I saw your colors and must confess to my surprise. I thought you were John's man."

"Not since Bouvines," Berkshire responded.

"I would speak with you, Lord Stanton." Terric clasped his brother on the shoulder then, telling him without speaking what would happen next.

"About Roysa? You've my approval, brother. Though you do not need it."

"No," he agreed. "I do not. But am glad for it anyway. 'Tis a decision that may well alter both my course and your own." He watched as injured men continued to be carried past them through the courtyard, wishing to say more. To tell Rory he may well stay here, at Dromsley, relinquishing his position as chief to his brother. But he needed to know Rory was, indeed, ready.

"I will finish here," Rory said.

Terric nodded his thanks.

Once he and Stanton were separated from the others, Terric didn't hesitate. It would be a long night, and much needed his attention. "What happened?"

"I fell ill," Stanton began. "I thought to send the men ahead but did not trust any to lead the group in my stead."

An affliction Terric could understand.

"When I came upon Ulster's men, I could not get a message through. I would not have attacked, but it became necessary."

"You were spotted?" he guessed.

"Aye. By then, the only message was my captain's dead body and the hope that you'd be reinforced enough to engage." Stanton crossed his arms. "You were under siege."

"We were."

Stanton did not ask about the change in his plans.

"Thank you for your assistance."

"And for yours."

Terric might have chosen siege, but a quick victory was always preferable. With the help of their allies, they had accomplished just that with minimal loss of life.

Except for Gilbert and several others.

Terric clenched his fists. King John was playing games with them. The order needed to meet again, to discuss their course of action.

"We will likely be going to war against the king."

"Aye," Stanton agreed.

"One that could be drawn out for years."

Again, his ally agreed.

"Then there is no reason to wait. No time will be better."

"For?"

He should ask the man for permission. He'd surely give it, considering he'd already granted Terric's request to court his daughter. But he would take no chances, including giving Stanton the opportunity to say no.

"To marry your daughter."

Stanton's eyes widened.

"Tomorrow."

CHAPTER 39

"T was a bit strange having a wedding amidst so much death."

Roysa had a difficult time believing she had just walked into *her* chamber, with *her* husband.

"Unfortunately, death will be our constant companion these next few months. Or even years." Sadly

Squatting in front of the hearth, Terric tended to the fire, having relieved the chambermaid. Though thankfully not the one who fancied her husband. She was one person Roysa would not miss when they finally left Dromsley.

"To think, I did not like you."

Roysa liked him very much now. He wore nothing but a long linen shirt, one she was eager to remove.

Because it was her wedding night, Idalia had insisted on helping Roysa dress in the lady's chamber, as if she were not capable of doing so with her own maid.

Once Idalia had left, satisfied with her appearance, Roysa had opened the door connecting her chamber to that of her husband—this, she knew, would be her true chamber. Terric had just been crouching down to the fire. Two goblets of wine awaited them, though she had eaten and drunk her fill at their wedding feast.

The one that had also served as a victory celebration. Unlike this morn, when they had buried the fallen, including Gilbert, the mood at their wedding had been almost lighthearted.

Wives and their children had been brought back into the castle, and the only evidence of the short siege and ensuing battle was the large bump on Terric's head, which could be felt though not seen. And the freshly dug graves. Even her father had smiled more than normal, his acceptance of her new status coming much more easily than she would have expected.

Her father had posed only a half-hearted objection last eve, saying her mourning period was not yet over, but Terric had declared firmly, "'Tis over."

Not the flowery proposal the old Roysa would have liked. But she'd learned not to place too much value on appearances. Although she'd never expected her second wedding would take place on the same day as a funeral . . .

Naught mattered except her very handsome husband, who stood and made his way toward her.

"Do you think it odd," he said, slipping his finger down to the sole tie on her shift. Pulling it, he let the two long strings hang down. "That we are man and wife?"

Her core began to pulse.

She wanted him to kiss her. Now.

"And not one time . . . ," Terric continued.

He didn't kiss her, as she'd hoped. Instead, Terric lifted his shirt over his head, standing gloriously naked in front of her. The fire's light flickered on his backside, and Roysa was sure she'd never seen anything so appealing in her life.

"Did I . . ."

He gripped the sides of her soft linen shift and lifted it over her head, letting it drop to the floor. One more step, and they would be touching.

"Tell you . . ."

She couldn't help but look down. Terric, hard and obviously quite ready, still did not touch her. Roysa could not seem to move herself.

When he did take a step, she did the same—although she moved backward. Right up against the door.

"That I love you."

Her heart skipped a beat.

"Do you say it now?"

Terric reached over and ran his fingers down her arm.

"I thought to show you."

She swallowed. "Aye?"

Terric nodded slowly, his hand moving over her hip now.

"Aye."

When it moved to her inner thigh, Roysa struggled to stay standing.

"I've something to confess," she managed.

His fingers moved closer. So close.

"I already know."

His fingers entered her then, and Roysa could feel the throbs of pleasure coming already. With just that one touch, she exploded, crying out his name.

One moment, she was against the door, standing of her own volition. The next, Terric had hiked her legs on each side of his body, lifting her up from the floor.

He guided himself inside, and kissed her. Hard.

She didn't care that the wood scratched her back. Or that it must be hurting him to hold her up this way. Roysa cared only about the sweet sensation of his hips and mouth moving in tandem.

No sooner did the climax abate than Roysa felt it building again.

Harder and harder he pumped, and she held on until . . .

"Roysa," he breathed. And with a final jerk, he cried out her name. Again she came, panting and attempting to say his name in return. Nothing came out but "T—"

Leaning his head back just enough that she could see his face, Terric moved a strand of hair away from her eyes, smiling. "I love you."

EPILOGUE

"**Y**ou're looking at me oddly."

Terric chuckled, wishing Roysa were riding with him as she'd done the past sennight. He'd even considered leaving her horse at the last manor they've visited. The only reason he had not was because Roysa seemed partial to the mare.

They'd been riding all day, their pace slowed by the mud that had resulted from the snowmelt. Much too long for him not to feel her. Touch her. Make love to her as he'd done every day since their quick wedding weeks ago. Thankfully, Licheford Castle finally rose up ahead of them.

Terric looked back. Lance and Idalia rode side by side behind them, and his clansmen followed his two friends. Nay, he corrected himself. No longer friends. His brother and sister through marriage.

He was looking forward to seeing the look on Conrad's face when he learned of it.

"Why?" Roysa asked.

"Why do I look at you oddly?"

The sight of Roysa rolling her eyes at him made him grin. "Nay, why do the clouds insist on dropping rain on us every single day?"

It was one of the things he enjoyed most about

her. That she could ask such questions without even the hint of a smile. "Of course I want to know why you are looking at me so oddly."

"I looked at you that way," he explained, slowing his mount in response to the horse's cues. The terrain was, indeed, becoming rockier. "Because I was remembering the day we met."

Roysa hated being reminded of it, which was likely the reason he did it so often. When her eyes flashed in mock anger, she said all manner of things. Many of which made him laugh. And with all that was happening around them, Terric needed to laugh.

"I really did dislike you."

Roysa's eyes narrowed. "I believe I disliked you more."

He pretended to consider it. "No, that could not possibly be true."

Her mouth dropped. "You . . . you, sir, are a boar."

"And you, my lady, are unkind."

"You are both making our heads ache," Cait called from behind them.

"Fair payment for the worry you've caused."

When he looked back, his sister scrunched her nose in annoyance.

Well, if she was annoyed, he was more so. He hadn't wanted her to come along—and Rory had agreed with him that it was much too dangerous for her to attend the order's meeting at Licheford Castle. Of course, she had proceeded to recruit Roysa and Idalia to her cause. They'd insisted that if it was safe enough for them to attend the meeting, surely Cait could go too. A logical argument, and so he had agreed—on the condition that she would explain why she had come to England after all these years.

Cait had said something about it being her fight too, and Terric had nodded, knowing right along it was a lie. Roysa had argued it didn't matter—she was accompanying them, and that was that. And so she had.

Terric wrapped the leather reins around his hands and looked up at the castle they approached—an even more impressive structure than Dromsley.

"I don't think I've ever seen a castle so big," Roysa said as they approached the enormous gatehouse.

"Are you speaking to me?" he asked her playfully. "I thought you were vexed at my recounting of our meeting," he teased.

"I am vexed," Roysa admitted. "And will be vexed every time you mention that very unfortunate incident."

On this, he disagreed. "Unfortunate?"

The men who'd ridden ahead of them were already speaking to Licheford's guards.

"'Twas one of the most fortunate days of my life, finding Idalia's sister battling with my guards. I just did not realize it then."

Though she laughed, Terric did not. In this, he did not jest. He loved her so much, it was not natural. Surely no one person should dominate one's thoughts in such a way. Especially not as the order prepared to declare war against the king.

"Mine as well," she said, her horse dancing under her.

Dammit.

He dismounted, less inclined to get through Licheford's gates than he was to touch his wife. Handing his reins to Rory's squire, the one his brother had insisted on bringing so he could get the experience he needed, Terric reached her in just a few strides. She seemed to understand his intent and began to dismount as he got to her.

"They will tease me for this," he said, "but I don't care."

When her arms encircled his waist, Terric wondered briefly how he had allowed hate to rule him for so long. This, Roysa's love, was much, much sweeter.

The men cheered when he kissed her.

"I didn't expect to find a lusty Scotsman at my gates."

He took his time breaking apart from his wife, finally turning toward the voice. Toward Conrad, the man who had begun this rebellion and who would help guide them through its darkest days.

His friend looked every bit as shocked as Terric had expected. But Conrad wasn't looking at him or Roysa. Following his gaze, Terric finally realized who he was staring at.

And why his sister, after all these years, had returned to England. *Cait*

⚜

LOOK FOR CONRAD'S STORY IN THE EARL, THE final installment in the Order of the Broken Blade series, coming 2020.

BECOME AN INSIDER

We may not be knights intent on toppling a monarchy, but the Blood and Brawners are certainly one fun group of romance readers who enjoy being teased (actually, that drives them crazy but I do it anyway) and chatting all things romance reading and hunky heroes.

Facebook.com/Groups/BloodandBrawn

Not on Facebook? Get updates via email by becoming a CM Insider. Delivered bi-weekly, this includes "My Current Obsessions" as well as sneak peeks and exclusive giveaways.

CeceliaMecca.com/Insider

ABOUT THE AUTHOR

Cecelia Mecca is the author of medieval romance, including the Border Series, and sometimes wishes she could be transported back in time to the days of knights and castles. Although the former English teacher's actual home is in Northeast Pennsylvania where she lives with her husband and two children, her online home can be found at CeceliaMecca.com. She would love to hear from you.

Made in the USA
Columbia, SC
06 November 2019